Gold Coast Anthology: UNDERTOW

"Tales from Outside the Flags"

Gold Coast Anthology:

UNDERTOW

Prana Press

Cover Art & Interior Illustrations by Shauna O'Meara

Prana Press
Gold Coast,
Queensland,
Australia

www.PranaWriters.com

National Library of Australia Cataloguing-in-Publication entry
Title: Gold Coast Anthology / editor Prana Press

ISBN-13: 978-1-936884-10-0

TABLE OF CONTENTS

FOREWORD

Louise Cusack

Who doesn't love short stories? I remember as a ten-year-old, staying up past my bedtime with a torch under the mosquito net reading them. The house was dark around me while I was completely immersed in the science fiction futures of Isaac Asimov or the whimsy of Roald Dahl. When I was older I fell madly in love with Edgar Allan Poe, and adored his use of language. Only Poe could succumb supinely to imperious domination. When I was a few years older again I read Anaïs Nin's evocative 'Little Birds' and was shocked by how deliciously wicked her tales were.

Short stories bring out the voyeur in most of us. They feel like a tiny window into someone else's life, like witnessing an argument, or a kiss, leaving you wanting to know more about those people and their lives. Inside the pages of this anthology you will meet fascinating characters and explore several genres, all with the unifying theme of a single region—the enigmatic Gold Coast. For me, growing up in suburban Brisbane, the Gold Coast was a mysterious world of glamorous meter maids in their gold bikinis, endless palm trees, sundrenched beaches that smelt of coconut sun-tanning oil, and the cool dark caverns of clubs and pubs where people retreated from the heat. Since those carefree days of the sixties and seventies, the region has evolved through phases of rampant development, tourism, crime and cultural change. I can think of no other place to rival the Gold

Coast for complexity, and these stories so clearly reflect that.

In fact, my own complex interaction with the Gold Coast began five years ago when I was contracted to teach a series of writing workshops to a group of sixteen aspiring novelists at Broadbeach Library. In my role as a writing teacher and mentor, and as a published author myself, I've had the privilege of working with a great many writers to help them hone their skills, but I could feel straight away that this group was special. For a start they were chosen from a Gold Coast-wide writing competition as the best of the best, so they had talent in spades. But it was their dedication to publishing success and their commitment to help each other that really impressed me, especially as that first year wore on. They all wrote in different genres (romance, crime, children's fiction, science fiction, literary fiction) but that didn't seem to matter. They were all intent on bettering their skills. And sharing! Their work. Critiques. Publishing opportunities. Encouragement. Enthusiasm. Commiseration when someone had a story rejected by a publisher. Celebration when stories were sold. By the end of the year they'd formed into a solid unit—the Prana Writers—and since that time they've built on their successes, relied on each other's strengths, and created a safety-net of support for when self-doubt comes calling. In that environment they've gone on to sell novels and countless short stories, win competitions and garner awards.

These productive wordsmiths, the Prana Writers, also share their knowledge and support with other writers in the region. The anthology you are holding contains not only their own work, but the stories of other talented Gold Coast writers. I know you will enjoy reading it, and I hope that a sprinkle of the Prana Writers' magic rubs off on you, inspiring you to excellence and generosity in whatever passion you pursue.

PREFACE

Creating an anthology, especially for the first time, is really like stepping off a precipice into the unknown. Not that you can quite believe it up front, but at this end of the experience it is clear how innocent we were of the task that lay before us. Jung's 'fool' archetype comes to mind. The trick of taking the leap of faith is about enjoying the free-fall rather than fearing it and trusting that it will be all fine in the end.

This is made much easier if you know you have support - and we had that in spades. Here's a shot at acknowledging those generous people, groups and organisations that guided us through the various steps, woven into the story of how the anthology's came to be.

This began as a Prana Writers (PWs) concept initiated by myself, inspired by my work and passion for the Gold Coast's Heritage. It was the start of April 2013. There was less than a month to get an RADF grant application together, and so Prana Writers (PWs) started running, and haven't stopped since! A key supporter was Kyla Stephan, along with the staff at the Gold Coast City Council Local Studies Library. They were keen to have the collection 'reinvigorated' by our stories - particularly for photos where the details had been lost to time. We engaged an editor and publisher to mentor us through the publishing process. Helen Stubbs also provided editing services and assisted in getting the anthology off the ground.

Before the grant was approved we set up a Facebook page, Twitter account, and started sifting through photos. Early June we received the RADF grant from the Regional Arts Development Fund jointly funded by Gold Coast City Council and Arts Queensland. It took us only ten days from grant approval to opening submissions with myself pulling the website together, the Local Studies Library helping us finalise the 100 photos and getting copyright clearance and Kay Gibb preparing the submission guidelines.

The photos were a key feature. The set of just over 100 were drawn from the local collection, 'Picture Gold Coast', and authors were invited to select one or more photos which inspired them. We'd like to make special mention of local photographer, Ray Sharpe, whose photos proved most popular with the authors. His chart topper being 'Snapper Rocks', featured in Elli Housden's story, *Snapper Rocks*. The photo that inspired the author leads each story and there is a beautiful index in the back that gives you more information about each image.

Many supported us in getting the word out — in particular Queensland Writers Centre and just about every writers group around Australia we could think of. Things were pumping and we were averaging 100 hits a day on our website. We were grateful for interviews by Max Webber, ABC FM Gold Coast and Jason Nahrung for writing an article in the QWC monthly mag.

All the PWs helped review the submissions and gave input on the selection process. We thank EVERY author who took the time to submit a story. It was an inspired collection of stories.

The editing period was an intense time between editors and authors. We are grateful for the advice of Michael Aird, for advice on aboriginal matters broached in the story *Jumpinpin* and the Quanda-mooka legend.

We did have some difficulties over the inclusion of photos in the anthology, and were very grateful for the assistance of Brett Kiellerop and David Morris of Brevid Books who assisted us through the process of publishing. This is also where the graphic design skills of our own J. S. Choinski came to the fore in typesetting and formatting our little volume and doing an exceptional job of including the photos, preparing galleys, making corrections and as frontline proofer. PW David Stringer carefully proofed the volume assisted by myself and PWs Penner and Rebecca. Paul Garrety provided editing services during the publishing stage. Kay Gibb meanwhile did an incredible job drafting and sending out contracts with authors and artist Shauna O'Meara.

Great segue into a special mention of the work of Shauna on the cover art—which manages to reflect (literally) the Gold Coast itself and the menace of the 'Undertow'. I hope you notice the clever micro images within her artwork. There is a unique image for each story, and you will see they have been used as the scene breaks with each story.

The timing of writing this preface precludes us from naming those involved in the final marketing stages of the anthology - but we do thank you. PW Rebecca Fraser has been leading the social media charge the whole way through the anthology and will lead that to the end, I am sure. There are others too who did not want to be mentioned, but we are grateful to your contribution to the making of this anthology. Special mention though to Louise Cusack, for her ongoing encouragement, support, advice, and wonderful Foreword.

Finally a note about the stories included here. The terms of the RADF grant were to support the emerging talents of the PWs, while drawing on the talents of experienced writers connected with the Gold Coast. Ten of the story places were reserved for PW stories while the other ten were put to open submission. You will find a range of genres and styles, as well as authors at difference stages of their writing journey.

Do enjoy this collection, whether you read from cover to cover, or dip into stories or photos that appeal. We hope you gain a sense of what the essence of the Gold Coast was, is or might become. It is a multifaceted city, and our stories reflect that: the boom and bust mentality in *Lions in Autumn*, sexual tension in *The Clearing*, impacts of war in *Dear Sam*, *Duck* and *War Bride*, a watery future in *Paradise Drowned* and *Deliver Me*, through to the philosophical stories of *Three Wishes* and *Last Day at Elephant Rock*. Always, always there is the ocean, ebbing and flowing through stories like *Coralesque*, *That Girl No More*, *Snapper Rocks* and *No Lime Ice Cream*. Ghosts walk the stories in *Jumpinpin* and *Breath*. Gold Coast tourist spots feature in *Pulped Fiction* set at Coolie Rocks and *Frangipanis* with memories of feeding the lorikeets at Currumbin. *The Ghosts of Our Ancestors*, takes us back in time to the white settlers. Wider issues are also covered, with *Empty Calories* taking a look at school bullying and *In the End* delving into assisted suicide. Of course there are many layers to the stories, that take them beyond the Gold Coast, touching on love, death, life, and the future we are creating. All great stories, making it all too easy to get caught in the *Undertow*. Relax into the anthology - let the currents take you...

-   Project Coordinator, Janis Hanley

The Prana Writers, Gold Coast Anthology 2014
Tom Betts, J. S. Choinski, Penner Choinski, Rebeccca Fraser, Paul Garrety, Kay Gibb, Janis Hanley, David Stringer, Nicola Tierney

NO LIME
ICE CREAM

Betsy Roberts

The smell of grilling hamburgers hangs in the air over everything, always, but on really hot, busy days, it fights with the sweet rush of malted milk and the strawberry ice cream and the salty sweat of sun burnt kids and grinning surfies. All those white teeth, tanned faces and peroxide hair—your group.

"Hey Shirley, give us a Coke and a Dagwood? Can I pay ya next time? Wallet's back in the sheds." Shorty's wallet is never where it needs to be.

Shirley flicks him a knowing look and raises an eyebrow. She swirls a skewered saveloy through the yellow batter, swoops it across to the deep fryer, wipes her hands on her apron and turns. It's almost a single motion. That might be about the thousandth Dagwood Dog she's served.

"I said, 'last time,' last time, Shorty," says Shirley. "You're lucky Jack's not here. You know you'd never get away with it." But she's grinning at him, at all of you, and already laying out buns and flipping onion rings and patties on the sizzling hotplate. She knows what everybody wants and she knows Shorty will pay when he can.

There's a skinny freckled kid with a white zinc nose scuffing his feet on the sandy floorboards, not game to push past your group—the big boys, the really cool Headland Surfies.

"Let that littlie through, boys," she says.

"What you want, sweetie?"

She leans over the counter and he mutters something, but it's lost in the babble of the lunchtime crowd and the Beach Boys on the jukebox and the high-pitched whine of the milkshake machine. She catches sight of Carol, who's meant to be helping me, but has found something much more urgent to do out at the tables.

"Carol, you've wiped that table dry," Shirley's voice rises above it all. She probably can't even whisper quietly any more. "Do your flirting later. Come and see what this little kid wants."

I was hoping Carol would come back to the milk bar counter. I could've gone to lunch. I could have gone to hide. I know you're there with Shorty and Des and the others. I saw you come in, but I tried not to stare. And now I'm serving a mum with what seems like a hundred kids who all want different sorts of ice cream, so it's easy to pretend. That I didn't see you.

We've just got a new flavour to add to the half dozen ice cream varieties we have to rattle off every time a customer asks for a cone: Coconut Ripple. Jack's been talking it up over the loud-speakers, and it's pretty popular. The mother thinks they'll all want that, but one little rebel turns his nose up when he sees what his sister's getting.

"Yuk, it looks like someone stuck bubble gum in there. I want lime."

But there isn't any lime today.

"I'm sorry," I say. If you only knew how sorry. "There's chocolate; or raspberry ripple. Or passionfruit, that's nice."

"Pooey," says the kid, and turns to his Mum. "Why haven't they got lime?" He's not quite shouting, but it's loud enough that people are starting to turn around and look. And by now I know you and the boys are watching as well.

It's a game. All I have to do is glance up and give you a look, a smile. It wouldn't kill me. But I can't. I can't play properly. Carol's good at it. I can hear her now, her and Shorty. She can talk to everyone and make jokes and laugh, and if one of the guys asked her out she'd go, or if she didn't want to, she'd say 'no' and the world wouldn't fall in.

For as long as I can remember, well, since I first saw you come in, with those green eyes and your eyelashes stuck together with salt, and that smile, I've been watching. Been spinning fantasy conversations and encounters in my head, but doing everything to avoid the possibility. And now it's me you're watching, and my face is burning and my hands feel as though they won't be able to work the ice cream scoop.

You came into the kiosk by yourself one day.

"There's a dance at the Surf Club," you said. Carol was serving you, but I was wiping down the tables and you came and asked me if I'd like to go. I didn't even know you knew my name, but you said Shirley had told you.

"I can't really," I said. How pathetic. I didn't even give any reason.

"Did Garry ask you out?" Carol said when I went back behind the counter, "Neat, eh? Where're you going?" And when I told her I said 'no,' she said, "You're mad. You really like him, don't you?"

"Yes," I said, "I do," but then it got busy and I couldn't even

3

put into words for myself exactly what I thought might happen if I let myself say 'yes,' so there wasn't any point trying to explain it to Carol. But I hoped she'd tell them that I do like him. It's easy for her, working here all the time. I'm away in term time, then it's like I'm the new kid behind the counter again at the start of every school holidays.

And back in the real world, little Mr Picky's mother is saying, "Come on Mark, what about a milkshake? They've probably got lime milkshakes," and he says, no—actually, he yells, "I don't want a milkshake, I want an ice cream!"

"Well, you can have chocolate and be happy with that," she says and gives him a bit of a clip around the ears, "and you can stop that this minute, or I'll give you something to cry about!"

Because the other kids have all started complaining too. "I'm itchy, Mummy, Mine's melting! Come on, Mark. Make him hurry up, Mum!"

But I've promised myself that next time you ask me out, I'll say 'yes'. Because last week when I was riding home, you just rode up next to me on your bike, like that. There we were; talking about nothing much, like normal people. That is, after me nearly falling off my bike from shock and embarrassment. But we'd laughed about that too. We were regular friends for a while, until we got to your street, and it was so good. I felt as though I could be anyone, and that all those romantic stories I imagined might not always just be fantasies.

Today the surf's pretty crappy though—north-easterly—so you'll probably be gone by the time I finish work. Not much chance of a quiet bike ride for two.

My counter's really busy now, but Carol's actually come over from the grill counter to help me. The lime ice cream kid's mother is trying to sort out whether she's got stuff for everyone or forgotten something for whoever's back down the beach under the umbrella—god forbid there are more of them—and all you guys are heading this way.

I can hear Shorty stage-whispering, not so quietly to Carol, "Some lime ice cream would really hit the spot, love."

She's giggling. "Shut up, Shorty."

The mother finally hands me the money, and I look up as I'm turning round to the cash register, give everyone a grin, but try to make it a quick, special smile for you. Shorty says, "Hey, Janet," and you and a couple of the others give me a nod.

I'm almost finished serving the family from hell and then someone else is asking what sort of ice-blocks we've got. But there's a conversation happening along the counter from me now that I can hear snatches of but I think I don't want to hear any of it, ever, and I turn around just in time to see Carol handing you your malted milk with extra ice cream, and to hear you saying to her, "So I'll see you about seven, then?"

She smiled at you from under those long eyelashes and said, "See you then, Garry."

The others all clapped you on the back and looked like they were laughing and shouting, but I couldn't hear what they were saying. My mouth felt as if it had forgotten how to move. And you didn't look at me when you went back out to the surf sheds with your caramel malted milk and your well-done hamburger with cheese, no onion.

CORALESQUE

Rebecca Fraser

There was a time when surfing was my life. Heck, it was more than that, it was my religion. I surfed the breaks at dawn, and returned to chase barrels again at dusk. The ocean's salt-white tightness drying on my skin felt more familiar to me than the suds of the shower that cleansed it away. I was good too. I guess we all were, really. Skegs, we were known as back then. You don't hear the term so much these days.

Hang around the beaches enough and you get to know each other's styles and boards. If you weren't in the surf, then you were watching other surfers, scrutinising their moves; checking out technique. That's how Saxon first caught my eye. I know I said I was good, but if you put me up against Saxon then I looked pretty clumsy. He was a dead-set natural. Could carve it up on his McCoy like no-one else. In the water that weathered board of his was like an extension of his body, all grace, guts and harmony. He could've easily gone pro, but he wasn't interested in anything like that.

"I just want to keep it for myself, man," he said to me once, as we sat on the beach at Kirra, our wetsuits pulled down to our waist. "D'ya know what I mean?"

He looked at me, rum-coloured eyes hidden beneath a shag of long brown hair—a beached-up Slash of *Guns n Roses* fame.

Of course I knew what he meant.

We became pretty tight, Saxon and me. As tight as you could get with someone like Saxon, that is. We were all chasers back then: chasing beer, chasing waves, chasing girls and a good time. But Saxon, he marched to the beat of a different drum.

He occasionally came out with our group—well, my group really—but he didn't rage like the rest of us. Sometimes, if I badgered him enough, he'd come to *The Playroom* and listen to a band. He was usually happy to sit at one of the sticky, wooden tables, hiding behind his hair while we all slammed about on the dance floor. One time, get this, we went to see the *Hoodoo Gurus* play. I lost sight of Saxon in their second set. You know where I found him? He was outside, sitting on the bank of Tallebudgera Creek, staring up the moonlit estuary to where the surf rolled in alongside Burleigh Headland.

"You okay, man?" I asked. "They're gonna play 'Wipe Out' soon. Don't wanna miss that." My voice was clumsy with beer.

"Check the surf out, Brett," Saxon said. "It's pumping."

It was indeed pumping, but not as hard as the *Gurus*, so I left him to it. I looked back across the car park before I rejoined my mates, and that's how I like to remember him best. A broad-shouldered silhouette, sitting at peace, looking out to sea.

I was studying Law in those days. Bond University had only been open for a couple of years, and it was a pretty big deal to have a place there. Between lectures and a part-time job at the Pancake Palace, I still managed to get a surf in most days.

Saxon had a permanent gig at a local screen printing business just over the border. He liked it well enough. He was good at colour matching and that sort of thing, and it was close to his little apartment in one of those old sixties walk-ups behind Rainbow Bay.

I met up with him at least a couple of times a week. We went wherever the surf was peaking, but favoured the southern end of the Coast: Snapper Rocks, Kirra, D'bah, all the usual haunts.

Life was good. I was starting to pull some decent grades at Uni, I had a top bunch of mates, and things were looking pretty good between me and Louisa-with-the-legs at the Pancake Palace. I'd just gotten rid of my old Escort in favour of a Sandman and, between it all, there was surfing, the backbeat to my existence.

But then Saxon changed.

If I had to pinpoint where it started, then the storm was the beginning. January storms are a given in Southeast Queensland, but that monster of nineteen ninety-one was a real doozy.

We were sucking back a few cold ones on Saxon's balcony when it rolled in. Grey-green clouds united at the horizon and drew themselves like a static sheet across the blue afternoon sky.

An electric calm settled, and Saxon tipped the neck of his beer at me; we both knew what would follow. When the first thunder crack came my eardrums bellowed right along with it. It boomed just over our heads, singeing the air. Then the rain. Sub-tropical, pregnant drops that thudded to the ground sporadically at first, then quickly built momentum. The storm engulfed the day and we relished it.

"Surf'll be huge tomorrow." Saxon smiled around his beer.

And it was.

The storm cell brought with it a huge swell, with challenging conditions up and down the Coast. A gale was still blowing when I pulled up at Burleigh Headland that morning. White caps foamed and furied and a little mouse of excitement scampered in my guts at the sight of the pounding surf. Past the second break some of the waves were twelve-foot boomers.

I waxed up and swung my arms impatiently. I could always meet Saxon in the water, but I said I'd wait for him. I stood beneath the Norfolk Pines and surveyed the beach. It had been officially closed due to dangerous conditions. A lifeguard patrolled up and down, buggy tyres churning through meters of brown foam that whipped and frothed at the shoreline. The usually pristine beach was littered with all manner of detritus—logs and fence posts, palm fronds and husks, plastic bags, long strands of russet seaweed, a lone rubber thong. With each tidal surge, more debris was pushed up the foam-flecked sand. The clean-up job would be huge.

"Let's go, Brett, you big girl." Saxon, flicking at my rear with his leg rope. I turned to give him a shove, but he danced out of reach, an excited puppy.

"You ever surfed waves like this?" I asked him.

"Only in my dreams, bro." His eyes gleamed. "Hoist up those petticoats, dude, it's going to be bitchin' out there."

"Get stuffed," I replied good-naturedly.

We picked our way from the top of Burleigh Hill down through the National Park to where the best surf could be accessed a short distance from the beach. It was a trickier route than entering from the sand, but expended a lot less energy than paddling beyond the headland. Several other surfers were making the pilgrimage and banter was high as we jostled between pandanas palms to access the rocky path to the base of the cliff.

A brush turkey swaggered and scratched to our left, his red and yellow markings vivid between the lantana which gave way to a clear view of the black lava boulders. The wind slapped us with a salt-wet sting as we navigated from one foam-slathered rock to the next, swaying for balance with every incoming wave. Timing is critical when you launch at Burleigh, you have to traverse the slippery boulders until you are in a position to leap into the sea with your board. I let Saxon go first and followed his gazelle-like leaping as best I could. With the next incoming wave we were off, paddling out with the backwash.

The next hour was exhilarating. The ocean ruthless, relentless, heavier; with more water and power in her barrels than I'd ever experienced. But, by God, it was fun.

Every now and then I'd catch a glimpse of Saxon, shredding all over the face of a fast, hollow wave. It was like he had a team of white stallions on a lunge rope, breaking one after the other. At one stage I saw him power down the line right next to me, his face contorted with rapture as he shot through the tube.

And then he got smashed. I saw his board fly up without him, and spin in the air as it descended. No biggie, we'd been axed several times that day, but I paddled towards him just the same.

There was blood. A lot of it. Saxon clung to his board. Crimson rivulets pulsed down his face, skewing his vision and tracking his cheeks. At first I thought the fin of his board had sliced his head, but when I pushed his hair back the jagged gash told a different story.

"Jesus," I breathed. "Saxon, we've gotta get you back, man." The shoreline rose and diminished with the ocean's swell. It seemed a very long way away.

"How bad is it?" Saxon asked. He had hauled himself back onto his board and was holding his hands to his head. "Shit, Brett, it hurts."

"Stitches, for sure," I said. "Let's go dude, hoist up those petti-coats."

Saxon laughed weakly. I winced as a fresh glut of blood spurted between his fingers.

I don't really remember how we got back to shore. When I try and recall it's all *blue-white, salt-breathe, dump-gasp, heart-beat, blood-swell, shark-smell, clamour-yammer, sand-stagger.*

Sand. Stagger. The beach beneath us. Saxon rolled off his board, pale and heaving and I looked around wildly for something to stem the flow of blood.

The lifeguard on his buggy, ahead in the distance. I jumped up, screaming and capering.

By the time he reached us, others had come, beach combers and surfing spectators; all advice and good intentions. An elderly sun-creased lady undid her tie-dyed sarong and knelt in her bathing suit to wrap it around Saxon's head. Rosettes of blood bloomed through the fabric and joined the rainbow of other colours.

The lifeguard was not much older than us. He radioed ahead to someone, somewhere, and I helped load Saxon on the seat next to him.

"Where are you taking him?" I asked.

"Southport. Gold Coast Hospital. They'll sort him out. What cut him? Fin? See that all the time."

"Nah, it wasn't the fin." I said, "It must have been something floating in the water."

"Wouldn't surprise me," the lifeguard nodded. "Look at the beach. All kinds of debris gets stirred up with a storm. Planks with nails in 'em, branches covered in barnacles, you name it. Seen a crate of coconuts washed up once, come all the way from Indo."

The buggy took off towards the Surf Club, and there was nothing left for me to do but gather up our boards, load them into the Sandman and head for home. I was exhausted.

I called the Hospital later that afternoon. A receptionist put me on hold and Bryan Adams filled the void. When she picked up again it was to inform me that Saxon was fine and could be picked up at any time. There wasn't anyone else, so I guessed that would be me.

"Eighteen stitches, man," Saxon said proudly. His head was swathed in white bandages turban-style. He wound down the car window and rested an olive-skinned arm. "You shoulda seen the shit that came out of it, Brett. Took 'em ages to clean it. Looked like coral shards. Reckon it might've been attached to some floating wood or something? It was pretty messy out there."

"Yeah, could've been," I agreed. Coral. Made sense, it was sharp enough. "You right to drive? I'll take you back to your car."

"Right as rain," Saxon said. We drove to Burleigh, reliving every moment of every barrel we'd caught that morning.

I hadn't heard from Saxon in three days, and I still had his board, so that afternoon I decided to drop it round. I took the three flights of stairs to his unit and rapped on the door. The blinds were drawn and it was unusually quiet. Saxon normally had a surf video playing, or *Triple J* blasting. I knocked again and called out. I was just about to leave, when the door opened a crack.

"Brett?"

"I've got your board. Want to hit Kirra?"

"Not today, I don't feel so good."

I pushed the door open and Saxon shrank back blinking as if the sunlight hurt his eyes. He'd removed the bandage. Even in the dim light of his unit, I could see the fever-red bulge of his wound.

"Dude, that doesn't look good." I flicked the light switch. "Let's have a look."

Saxon whipped his hands to his eyes. "Turn the light off, Brett."

I dragged him into the bathroom, turned that light on and prised his hands from his face for a better look. Saxon kept his eyes screwed tight against the glare and moaned as I inspected his head. The wound was angry and weeping, strained tight against the neat row of stitches. His head felt too hot, and looking at the scarlet lines that had started to thread from the gash, I felt hot too.

"Sax, you gotta go back to the doctor. It's infected. I had a mate, got blood poisoning from a nasty coral cut on his foot. Swelled up like a balloon. He got some penicillin; took care of it like magic."

"'kay. Just turn off the damn light." He shoved me hard. My hip bone connected with the towel rail.

"Jesus, Sax, take it easy." I rubbed at my throbbing hip.

"Turn off the fucking light!" His voice had a dangerous edge I hadn't heard before.

Wounded, I flicked the switch and left Saxon sitting in darkness on the edge of the bath. "I'll ring tomorrow," I called as I left. "Make sure you get to a Doctor." I banged the door a little on the way out, I admit.

I didn't ring Saxon the next day. I left it a couple of days, assuming the penicillin would kick in and douse his fever-temper with it. I was looking forward to a surf that afternoon so I called him first thing, before he would have left for work. The phone rang ten-eleven-twelve times before I hung up.

I tried him at work a little later that day.

"Saxon hasn't been in the last two days," his boss said. "Didn't even have the courtesy to call and let me know." An alarm bell clanged distantly in my mind. "Not like him, always been a bloody good worker. I expected better."

I tried Saxon again at home. With each unanswered ring, I felt my unease grow. That night after a double shift at the Pancake Palace, I blew Louisa off and drove to his unit. As before, the blinds were drawn. I knocked and waited. Nothing. I called Saxon's name. Nothing. But I could hear it. A squelching, laboured noise.

I threw my shoulder against the door until it gave. It was so dark and fusty inside at first my eyes didn't comprehend what they were seeing. Saxon was huddled in an armchair, but his head, something was wrong with his head. It was too big and lolled forward against his chest.

"Saxon?" My voice was air escaping from a balloon. I tried again, "Sax?" I hunkered down to get a better look.

The head lifted sluggishly and I fell back on my arse in shock and revulsion. Saxon was unrecognisable. His face obscured by gnarled cladding that started at the top of his head, and extended down his arms and torso and beyond. I noticed the fingers of one hand fused together in a misshapen clump. One bloodshot eye rolled at me, the other hidden altogether behind the barnacle-encrusted casing. The squelching noise began in earnest and I realised it was breathing. Dear God, Saxon was trying to breathe. A pendulum of snot swung from where the centre of his face should be.

"Jesus, Sax." I reached a tentative hand out and touched his shoulder. The growth was rough and cool. Coral. *It was coral.*

And it was alive and growing.

Saxon lurched at me with a wet growl. The weight of his encrusted body pinned me beneath him. I thrashed and screamed as the thing that had once been my friend snarled and gurgled on top of me.

With a mighty adrenalin-fueled thrust, I pushed him away and rolled, jabbering, against the couch.

The growling escalated.

I fled then, reaching the door in great, leaping strides, blood pounding in my ears. The last thing I saw was Saxon flailing on the ground. It was a pathetic sight. One or two remaining brown curls sprouted from his bulbous skull. His body, too melded together to use his limbs, rolled and snapped in an effort to get at me. I will always remember his remaining red eye fixed on me as I ran.

The sky was lightening as I fell upon the sparse patch of lawn in front of Saxon's unit block. I doubled over retching and sobbing. After I'd emptied my guts of the waffle stack I'd eaten what seemed like an eternity ago, I felt a little stronger.

I ran up and down neighbouring streets until I found a phone box, rummaged in my pockets for a coin, and dialed 000.

"What is your emergency, please? Police, fire or ambulance?"

In my shock I almost laughed. What was my emergency? How do you describe the fact that your mate has been overcome by a malevolent, fast-growing parasite?

"Ambulance," I said shakily. "My friend is…hurt." I gave Saxon's address, listened to the operator's questions and answered them as best I could. No, he's not bleeding. Yes, he is breathing…sort of. No, he couldn't talk. Yes. No. Don't know. *Just fucking get here.*

I returned to Saxon's units and hid behind the row of rubbish bins under the carport, hopping anxiously from foot to foot as I waited for the ambulance. Pairs of lorikeets nattered to each other overhead as dawn approached. An ambulance pulled up, and two paramedics got out. I heard their footfalls on the staircase and a door open on the top floor. Then, silence. I chewed at the skin around my thumb, ears straining. More foot falls. The paramedics returned. They were alone. Where was Saxon?

I crept from my hiding spot and moved behind a tenant's vehicle as the paramedics radioed in and caught snatches of conversation.

"…no, the unit was empty. Nothing to report. Where did the call come from? Not the unit? Public phone box. Right, must've been a prank. Bloody kids. Door was off its hinges though. Might pay to send a police car –"

The unit was empty? Where was Saxon? I had to see for myself.

I waited for the ambulance to leave, then climbed the stairs on shaky legs. The door was still ajar, and I pushed it open a crack, reached in and flicked on the light. Nothing. My heart thudded in my chest. I entered the unit and looked in each room. Empty. Only the eyes of numerous bikini centrefolds taped to the walls watched me. I made to leave, and then I saw them. Shards of coral, salmon-brown in colour littered the floor. A trail of sorts led to the front door, and a larger clump of the stuff lay just outside, as if it had scraped off on the door ledge.

I kept my eyes to the ground as I slowly made my way back down the stairwell. More shards. And over there, more. Every now and then, an ooze of mucus accompanied by a fetid saline stench. I followed the trail down the stairs, and across the street. It continued east, and suddenly I knew, and I was off and sprinting towards the beach.

A great furrow in the sand marked the labour Saxon had made to reach the ocean. In the dying of the night, I saw him for the last time. A giant misshapen slug, humping its way towards the water. There was nothing resembling humanity left. I sank to the sand, cold and damp through the knees of my jeans, and watched as the sea claimed my friend. It took a couple of surges, and then he was off with the backwash, just as we had been, two surfers with our boards, at Burleigh a week ago.

I remember sitting on the beach for a very long time. Morning rose about me, and the day began its routine. The breakers surged forward onto dawn-fresh sand. Walkers marched around me; a fisherman cast out not far from where I sat. Early morning surfers paddled out beyond the break, and I watched them, envying their carefree idealism.

LAST DAY AT ELEPHANT ROCK

Paul Garrety

When he asked me to spend the day with him I didn't realise he was dead.

Which, in hindsight, made his opening line *'I want to spend the rest of my life with you,'* redundant. At the time I just did what everyone else was doing and ignored him, leaving him stranded on the platform like a tall spindly tree, the flood of commuters flowing about him.

I boarded the 7.04 to Brisbane and sat down with the rest of the Grey People. That's what life is like without colour, and I was one of them, a grey could-have-been artist.

When I reached the street at Central he was on the pavement. Waiting. Smiling. A boy-man with black crinkly hair, white tombstone teeth and an angular face. Everything about him was long.

"Alicia," he said.

I stopped. It wasn't so much that he knew my name. It was more his voice. It was like recognising something I knew yet at the same time didn't. I looked at him, above the heads of people pushing past. He had green eyes. If they'd been any bigger he would have looked moronic, as it was they just bulged and burned.

He stepped forward hesitantly, holding a small bunch of violets in front of him like a talisman.

Violets were my favourite.

"I want to spend the rest of my life with you."

He said it in that half-in, half-out of memory voice.

"I – " I shook my head and ran.

When I stopped I found myself outside Hart and Brown, its familiar glass and brass solid and real. Far above, my small workstation beckoned, safe and numbingly secure. I sniffed and brushed my cheek with the back of my hand. It came away wet and smeary. I pushed through the revolving glass doors and into the lobby.

He was waiting by the elevators.

"Who are you and why the hell are you following me?" It came out hard and loud, my chin leading as always. Several people turned to look. He just cocked his head to the side and held out the violets.

"Come and have a coffee, Alicia, and I'll tell you. Ten minutes. Then if you want, go on up to your work and I won't bother you anymore."

I hesitated. There was a coffee shop in the lobby. I wasn't due to start until nine and, like always, I was fifteen minutes early.

"All right. Fine. Ten minutes. If you cause any trouble I'll call security, got it?" I held up my mobile, realising I had no idea how to call building security. He appeared to know it too because he was smiling again.

Somehow I ended up holding the violets.

"I'm Brett." He reached across the table, his hand huge and hovering. I hesitated, but finally took it tentatively. The touch points of his palm were roughened with calluses. That didn't seem to fit with the rest of him.

"I'm a gardener," he added and I felt my face flush. Most people identified themselves by what they did, didn't they? Alicia: graphic designer.

"Why are you following me?"

"Because I want you to spend the day with me."

"But who –?"

"Cappuccino?"

We looked up. A girl with a white shirt and black apron was holding two cups, looking down at us expectantly. I sighed and nodded.

"So the lemon juice and hot water must be for you," she said with a "'there you go."

Brett flashed her a lopsided grin and winked. She blushed beneath her acne and touched her hair before moving to the next table.

"Do I know you?" I tried again.

"Not yet, that's why I want to spend the day with you."

"Will you stop saying that!" I said too loudly, then quieter, aware that others in the coffee shop were pretending not to listen.

"Brett. Look, I'm flattered, truly I am. But I have to go to work and I really don't want you following me anymore. You're stalking me, did you know that?"

He sipped his hot water. Why would anyone pay three bucks for a cup of hot water and half a dried out lemon? He was watching me over the rim of the cup, his eyes huge.

"What if I told you I only had one day left to live and, of all the people in the world I would like to spend that day with, I've chosen you? Would you still prefer to just go to work?"

"Me? But why? You don't even know me, or more importantly I don't know who the hell you are. You could be some maniac. I mean, I don't know, do I? One day? Is that true?"

"Of course, otherwise I wouldn't have said it."

"So, sensible questions, first. How do you know my name? How do you know me at all?"

He grinned and sat back in his chair.

"I see you on the train all the time. I asked around, even followed you one day to see where you worked. So I guess for one day I did stalk you, but in the nicest way. I told myself—one day I want to meet that girl, talk to her. When I found out I was sick, I realised how much time I'd already wasted. So here I am, I want to do one thing that really matters every day I have."

"So, you may not only have one day left?"

"No, I may not, but then again, I may. It's hard to say, all I know is that I want to share this day, this minute, with you."

I spooned up some froth from the cappuccino, stalling. It was like arguing with myself. Part of me, the interred artist, intuitively—bizarrely—trusted him, somehow knew him at some level. But everyday, logical Alicia who craved normality and routine was running blind and scared in absolute denial.

I also knew whatever I did, whatever I decided right now, could never be undone. This was one of those defining life-choice moments that always seem so blindingly obvious later; a 'give way' sign I normally breeze through without looking.

The minute hand on the black and white clock above the counter clunked onto the twelve. It was nine o'clock. My mouth felt dry. I sucked at my lips tasting coffee and cinnamon, realising I'd also probably taken off what was left of my lip-gloss. Again. It was a nervous habit. A habit I instinctively felt he recognised. I straightened in the chair and picked up my mobile phone. I'd decided.

"So what do you want to do on your last day, then Brett?"

He pointed to a copy of an old black and white photo on the wall showing a small hut tucked into the lee of a huge rock, the ocean frothing around it.

"Let's go there."

We hired a car. It was one of those expensive sports jobs with leather seats, an electric soft top that folds itself up and a groin-jiggling growl. We drove top-down and fast all the way to Currumbin on the Gold Coast. Fortunately that morning I'd decided to bunch my wild gypsy curls into a ponytail, otherwise my hair would have ended up looking like his. Though the wind-blown "off-the-moor" look did kind of suit him.

We bought swimmers from the surf shop opposite the beach, loaded up with junk food and water and crossed the road to the sand. I wasn't normally a pink and green bikini girl, but today was way past normal. I reminded myself this was not a date, it was my charity act for the month. I was here to make someone happy, that was all.

I planned to stay in the open, around people. I might feel like I could trust him, but I wasn't completely insane either.

Everything felt good though: the sun, the frothy slurp of water around my ankles, even walking beside this strange man. I gave a couple of skips, scuffing the tidemark. "I'm so pleased I rang in sick today. It's just too beautiful to work."

"The day is simply a reflection of you."

I heard him, but pretended not to; pleased just the same. I pointed to the large glass and steel Vikings surf club, changing the subject. "There's your hut from the photo, looks like they renovated."

"You're right. Well, at least Elephant Rock is the same. Let's have our lunch on the other side of it. That way we can pretend the original hut is still there."

I hesitated. The beach on the other side of Elephant Rock was deserted. Some family groups were about twenty metres away on the Currumbin side—still close enough to call out to. I looked at Brett and he was smiling. I could swear he was reading my thoughts. I felt the blood rush into my face and as if in defiance of it led the way settling myself on the rocks beneath the look-out at the top of the rock, busying myself unpacking the food. Brett stripped off his shirt. He wasn't scrawny, more outdoorsy wiry. Hairy chest, but not a monkey back. I didn't do hairy like some women. No need for a scorecard here though, I reminded myself. He turned to look out at the sea before sitting down. He did have nice buns, though.

"I've never done anything like this, you know, Brett. Just gone off with someone I don't even know."

"But you do, don't you? Know me, I mean."

There it was again. Familiarity where there shouldn't be. I busied myself licking the chicken grease from my fingers.

"How could I?" I said finally. "But yes. At least I think so. God, that sounds so weird. Who the hell *are* you, anyway? Why do I feel I know you?"

He reached across and I felt his finger lightly wipe something oily from the corner of my mouth.

"Maybe we knew each other in a past life, or maybe you're just having a good time. It's what every day is supposed to be about, Alicia, valuing just this moment. Nothing makes us appreciate life more than seeing death approaching. So they tell me," he chuckled.

"But you look so healthy."

And it was true. Energy seemed to radiate from him. I couldn't believe he could be dying…well, any faster than the rest of us, anyway.

"Come on." He stood, his back to the sun, and held out his hand.

Sunlight streamed around him like a golden aura. I raised one hand to shade the glare, and allowed him to pull me to my feet with the other. After that it seemed the most natural thing in the world to just keep holding hands as we explored the rocks, the surf breaking around us.

There is talk and there is communication. Neither, in my limited experience, has much connection with the other. That day, though, Brett just seemed to know what I meant, despite what I said.

I'm not sure how we ended up at the Currumbin Bird Sanctuary in front of Holey, a 5.3 metre salt water croc. Like everything else that day it just seemed to happen.

"He's magnificent," I said reverently, "can you believe he's twenty?"

"Could you paint him?. Capture his pain?" he said, his hands clenching, eyes focused at some mid-point between it and us.

"Pain? What do you mean?"

"Maybe pain is the wrong word. It's like a buzzing tension. Can you feel it? His immense power overlaid with an intense frustration."

"Frustration? What do you mean?" I asked.

"At captivity." Brett turned to face me, eyes shining, boring into me. "You of all people must be able to imagine what it's like to be fully aware of what he was born to be, but tacitly accepting something less—simply to survive. The complacency of convenience."

"What would you have him do? Break out?" I said, my voice catching, thinking of my own glass enclosure back at Hart and Brown and the passionate fire that used to be my art, its fire damped long ago by practicalities.

Brett shrugged, "At least to try."

"And if he can't get out, what choice does he have then? He's trapped here, Brett."

"We always have a choice."

"And what about you? You said this is your last day. Is that your choice too?"

He just smiled and cupped my face with his large hands and kissed me in front of Holey.

I don't know what the name of the motel was. Our room had a TV, that may or may not have worked, a shower that definitely did and a bed. I remember the bed. Remember it gently supporting me as Brett slowly lowered me onto it. Felt it soft and cushiony against my back while his hardened hands explored my front, their callused roughness prickling goose-flesh in their wake. Finally, using its springs to meet his slow, languorous rhythm, lost in the moment, wondering if there would be others. Hoping for a tomorrow.

Later, in the small bathroom, the air still thick with trapped steam, I towelled off. The shower dripped, a staccato plip-plop in quick succession before pausing pregnantly, swelling, preparing for the next.

Plip-plop.

The words 'soul mate' danced lightly at the back of my head.

Plip-plop.

I was torn between anger and fear. Anger at having it all taken away almost before it started and fear at perhaps afterwards never knowing 'it' at all.

The door slid open, Brett came in and gently ran his fingers along the side of my face, smiling down at me.

"Almost ready?" he asked. "There's someone I want you to meet."

"This is the man I wanted you to meet," Brett said quietly.

Hospitals had always made me nervous, but until now I hadn't realised why. They were where people went to die.

We were standing at the end of a bed in a room of other beds. The man in front of us was connected by tubes and hoses to a number of ticking, clicking and pumping noises. His eyes were closed. He looked familiar.

"Who is he? I think I've seen him before."

Brett made a wry, pouting expression with his lips.

"He's an accountant, but for one shining moment he was a musician. Pretty good too. He used to catch the 7.04 to Central each morning, same as you; that's probably where you saw him. Always two rows back from the door, left hand seat, pretending to read a newspaper and desperately ignoring the music bubbling up within him. Here are some of his original scores."

Brett handed me a battered manila folder crammed with hand-inked sheet music.

A vague memory floated up of a sandy haired man—one of the greys on the train—a black leather briefcase balanced on his knees. I remembered catching him looking at me several times. He'd seemed...nice.

"What happened to him?" I said, voice hushed.

"It was the Numbers that killed him in the end, not the car."

"Is he dead?" feeling Brett's hand slip from my arm.

"Are you a relative?"

I jumped at the unfamiliar voice. A nurse stood beside me. Her face held a well-worn, caring expression.

"No. No, I, er, we –" I looked around for Brett.

"Brett?"

The woman was nodding and patting my arm.

"It's hard, but we have to let them go eventually, dear. Carbon monoxide poisoning is painless, but lethal. I've just received authorisation to turn off his life support. Poor dear has no family."

I backed away, shaking my head. "Brett."

I left her there, retracing my steps.

"Brett?" I moved faster. I heard the nurse call after me. I ran—out into the corridor, down flights of green lino stairs and through a set of swinging doors. I found myself outside, in a courtyard flanked by the low sandstone buildings of the hospital. I looked left, then right, unsure of where I was headed other than chasing the idea that I was running towards something.

Then I saw him. He was sitting on a bench seat facing a fountain, his head and shoulders bent, legs swinging lazily.

"Brett?"

He didn't look up. I walked over to him.

"Brett?"

The eyes were the same green but dimmer, like a verandah light left on outside a darkened house. His mouth lolled sloppily.

I eased myself down beside him and tentatively touched his shoulder. He jerked away.

"Are you all right?" which seemed so hopelessly inadequate when everything obviously wasn't, but it was all I could manage. All I wanted was for him to bounce to his feet, a big grin spreading across his face, half-scared I wouldn't forgive him for the cruel joke.

I waited for him to do that for a long time.

Finally, I heard someone approaching. It was another nurse.

"Oh, Michael. There you are. Do you know we've had the police out looking for you? How did you get down here? Come on, love, let's get you back up to your ward. I don't know, security in this place is a joke."

She eased the man up from the seat. Brett bumped into me but didn't glance in my direction.

"Wait." I called after them.

The woman turned.

"This man, you called him Michael?"

"Yes, he was admitted last week with concussion from Mersey, the care facility for the disabled—you know. He disappeared from his ward first thing this morning. Poor dear, he must have woken up and just wandered off, he has no idea really. It's a wonder he managed to dress himself much less anything else."

I went down to Mersey the next week, just to be sure. But Michael wasn't Brett. I knew he wouldn't be, not after I'd seen whose name was on the music scores. Oh, the body was the same, but the staff told me that Michael had never been able to look after more than the garden, and then only if carefully supervised. Brett had written the music and somehow his spirit had managed to both conduct and perform it, through Michael.

Two weeks ago 'Alicia, graphic design' would have said she'd imagined it. All of it. Even now it was hard to believe. And even if I had dreamed it, there were some things that remained. The memory of a man on a train hurtling down the wrong track. A man who, before forcing his own exit, paused to help me get off, no less finally, but unlike him, intact. I watched Michael for a moment more as he lovingly bedded in a new shoot then I bent down and kissed that memory hard on the cheek, feeling the confused green eyes watching me as I walked away.

I was already planning the palette mix for that green.

THE LIONS
IN AUTUMN

Tom Betts

Rowan put his hand on the metal latch. He thought briefly that this might not be a good idea, until he looked into the cage again. Pathetic.

He lowered his head, his grey beard rubbing the knot of his tie. *That idiot kid. Count on Greg to stuff things up. What is he to me anyway?* Rowan asked himself. What did you call the son of the woman you were sleeping with who wasn't your wife? Bastard-in-law?

Rowan tried to remember when he was twenty-one. Surely he was sharper back then. What year was that? It was a golden year, in the early fifties, the same year he loaded two longboards into his uncle's 1935 Terraplane sedan and headed north to the warmer surf of Queensland. He'd walked away from a law degree at Sydney Uni, or rather was pushed out the door for non-attendance. Pathetic. Just one of many bad decisions in his life.

He squinted against the sun as he looked across the sprawling expanse of drying, overgrown grass that surrounded him, over to a clump of trees a few hundred metres away. In the shade beneath them lounged the still figures of lions resting in the midday heat. One of them was up on its haunches, staring straight back at him. Something didn't look right. Rowan took a step in the lion's direction, his arthritic knee protesting. He took off his glasses and squinted harder. Then he saw it—the lion's chest was fluorescent red-orange, like a robin's breast. He shook his head.

"Get out here, you bastard," Rowan yelled at the demountable shack that served as his site office. It was the only structure for kilometres around. A lanky, young man stuck his head out the door, his prominent Adam's apple seeming to appear first. "You want me?"

"I called you, didn't I?"

The young man's long legs unfolded down the steps. His left boot raised a cloud of dust as it hit the ground.

"So, what do you think?" he asked through a proud, crooked grin.

"What I think, Greg, is that you need to have your bloody head read."

Greg's lips collapsed into a thin line. Even his shock of sun-blond hair hanging over his forehead seemed to slump.

"You said you wanted a lion, and I brought you a lion," young Greg said, his Adam's apple hammering like a piston.

"I'm talking about *that* lion," Rowan said, pointing at the clump of trees. "Are you colour-blind?"

Greg shifted uneasily. "No. Why?"

"Look at that artwork of yours. You ever seen a lion with a bright red chest before?"

"Yep. I got my inspiration from a picture in National Geographic,"

Greg said, leaving his mouth hanging open, as if in disbelief at Rowan's ignorance.

Rowan stared hard at the black void between Greg's teeth, trying to understand how someone so bereft of neural activity could find use for the word *inspiration*.

"Yeah, it was a great photo, mate. There was this red lion, sitting up just like that one, all proud-like, staring at the sunset on the cabana."

Rowan slowed his words with an effort. "You mean *savannah*?"

"Yeah, whatever."

"So, this photo of yours. It was sunset on the Serengeti, that sort of twilight colour where the sky turns the trees and landscape red everywhere?"

"Yeah, like I said it was a great photo."

Rowan shook his head and stared at his shoes. His face twisted as if wracked by pain. "You bloody idiot! It's eleven o'clock in the morning on a grassy wasteland outside Jimboomba, not some fucking *cabana*. That lion looks like a painted cardboard lion. You were supposed to make them look real. There's four million dollars' worth of Jap investors about to pull up here to decide whether to bankroll this lion park."

"What lion park?" Greg asked, standing his ground. "You've only got one real lion. The rest are make-believe, sitting under that tree."

"Exactly, Greg. Fake lions—yes, so the Japs can picture it, all right? I need their money and they want to invest it. Is it hard for you to understand? If the Japs think those lions are fakes, they'll think I'm a fake, and they'll drive away and this property will be worth –" Rowan stopped himself. "I need this to work. Do you understand?"

"What are you so dirty at me for?" Greg asked. "I drove all the way out to Toowoomba to bring you a real lion. You don't have to thank me or anything."

Rowan turned and looked at the cage. "A real lion?"

He walked over to the trailer, gripping his thigh with each painful step. "That?" he asked, pointing at the bloated mass of fur sleeping on the floor. Flies circled ulcers scattered across the lion's scruffy coat.

"This is a real lion, all right," he said. "A real sick, old, syphilitic lion. I'm surprised it survived the trip."

"He wouldn't give me a healthy one. Said you were s'posed to pay a thousand dollars hire fee. When I said you only gave me four hundred he gave me this one."

Rowan grimaced as if wracked by a migraine. He ran his fingers over his forehead then gripped his thick mane of grey hair.

Greg shifted uneasily. "He told me you're lucky you got this one, you cheap prick. He called you that, not me. And he wants it back by tomorrow night."

"Yeah, well, forget it, kid. If this is what we've got, then this is what we've got."

Greg followed Rowan's gaze to the lion in the cage. It snored; its pale, brittle hair cradling its head like a dirty pillow. It shook its fur with a half-hearted spasm.

"You mind if I go back inside?" Greg asked, pointing at the office, where an air conditioner's thermostat shuddered into high gear. "It's pretty hot out here."

Rowan ignored him.

"Okay, then," Greg said, and hurried back into the office.

Rowan took a cigarette from his pocket. He tapped the stick on his knuckle and flicked it into his mouth with practiced ease. The first cloud of smoke seared his throat and he exhaled it with more air than he needed.

He pressed his face against the cage.

"I don't know if the Japs are going to like you, Leo. But you're my last shot."

The lion's eyes opened, bright and alert, startling Rowan, then closed again and the snoring continued.

The door to the office flung open. "Phone call, Rowan," Greg called out. He hesitated for a second. "I think it's Mary. Your wife."

"I know who she is. Tell her I'll ring her back."

Greg nodded and retreated into the office.

Rowan turned back to the lion, sucking on his cigarette as he pictured what Mary would be doing right now. After hanging up the phone she would probably walk into the lounge room, past the photos of their two daughters and their three granddaughters.

She would settle into her padded chair, with her latest mystery novel and grab a chocolate macadamia from the lolly container shaped like a Bavarian dancer, complete with braces and a ceramic feathered hat for a lid. They bought it in Regensburg on their 'empty nest' tour of Europe after their youngest, Cindy, moved out of the house and settled in with her boyfriend, now her abusive ex-husband.

Mary's a good woman, has always stood by me, Rowan thought with a flicker of affection. Even when they almost lost the house and he had to take out another mortgage to cover his debts. If this lion safari didn't come off…. Never mind. Everyone thought Walt Disney was mad when he bought that orange orchard in Anaheim.

He wondered if lions were like pigeons and people, and mated for life. He couldn't remember if he had learned that at school. He didn't remember much at all. He was always too tired from waking up at 4:30 to train with the rowing crew.

"Rowan, you should be rowin'," was what his sports teacher, Coach White, told him in the tenth grade. He kept telling him so often that Rowan finally joined the crew, first in the eights then the quad sculls. He thought back to his early success in the sport—he was taller than most boys in Year 11 and his legs were steam engines, exploding with each stroke.

The coach loved him. Rowan's dad—well, he didn't exactly love him, but he seemed willing to notice him when he started bringing home trophies and ribbons, initially from the school, then the regionals, and eventually the state finals. He got his photo on the front page of the Newcastle Herald. It read: RAYMOND TERRACE LAD'S STROKE OF GENIUS

Then in Year 12 he blew his knee out and his times started to drag. Suddenly the gush of ribbons and awards and the letters from American universities dried up. His dad lost interest in him again, and Coach White stopped paying attention. Which was just as well, as he turned out to be a kiddie fiddler.

Rowan strummed his fingers on the cage wire.

Yes, Mary was a good woman, he thought. Even though he cheats on her. She knows about it, or does she? She never lets on, has never accused him. Ever.

And all the failed schemes. The real estate agency that went bust. The crayfish farm—what a debacle. And his attempt to launch competition against the Meter Maids—the Scarlet Starlets. He came up with that name himself. He coached them to learn cartwheels and do the splits as they made their way along Surfers Paradise beach promenade, handing out flyers for local beer gardens and 2-star restaurants. Rowan chuckled humourlessly at the memory. That cost a bundle. But he got some good gropes out of it, even a couple of roots.

What a good woman Mary is to put up with such a shit of a husband, he thought.

Rowan turned back to the sleeping lion. Its chest rose and fell like a ventilator diaphragm blowing air into a dying patient.

"What about you, Leo? Hey, big fella? You have a lady waiting for you back at that shithole of a zoo you live in?"

Rowan finished his cigarette and crushed it into the powdery earth. He looked across the property to its eastern border, then down at his watch.

Mango had assured him they would arrive at midday. They're pretty punctual the yellow bastards, he'd give them that much. Rowan flicked another cigarette into his mouth and hobbled over to a large bush.

He unzipped his pants and pissed on the shiny green leaves. The stream came in fits and grunts. Mary told him ages ago to get it looked at. He already knew his prostate was rooted. But he had no time to worry about the big C. He zipped up his pants and lit his cigarette.

The November sun cooked the grassy expanse around him, making the air above it shimmer and vibrate. Maybe through all the haze the Japs wouldn't notice the colour of that lion under the tree.

He looked to the west, where the haze was milkier above Lake Wyaralong and to the densely wooded hills on its north bank. He had a sudden urge to lose himself in that forest, never to worry again about mortgages, land deals, disloyal mates and idiot bastards-in-law.

He scanned the desiccated grass around him. Two hundred and forty acres of gum trees and stubbled clay. He turned to the cage. "You may be king of the jungle, but I've got more land here than Dreamworld."

He had picked the land up for a song—well, that and one hundred thousand Westpac Bank dollars. Queensland's Minister for Everything, Russ Hinze, had thrown him this bone in March after Rowan's former mate Syd McGuire had done the dirty and cut him out of the Princess Cove estate deal. Bastards, the whole lot of them.

Out of the corner of his eye, Rowan caught the first puff of dust. He leaned towards the driveway to get a better look.

"Yep, here they come, Leo." The lion didn't stir.

Rowan hurried over to his six-year-old BMW 316 and pulled his suit jacket off the passenger seat. He popped a mint in his mouth and checked his reflection in the dust-coated driver's side window, using his fingers to flatten his moustache and beard. His eyes shifted to the cut-outs of the lions shimmering under the distant trees, then up at a few bulbous clouds drifting towards the sun, threatening to cool the air.

"Fuck off," he muttered.

The door to the office opened. Greg pointed up the driveway. "Hey, Rowan. We've got company."

"Back inside," Rowan said. "And don't come out till they've gone."

Greg's shoulders slumped. Rowan stared at him until the young man pulled the door shut again. He limped as far up the driveway as his knee would let him, to keep the visitors well clear of the fly-blown cage.

A white Toyota Hiace van with tinted windows snaked up the driveway, dust leaping magnetically onto its shiny exterior.

Before the van stopped, the passenger door flew open and a round-faced Japanese man in his forties jumped out, planting his feet like a gymnast. He smiled broadly as he closed the upper button on his suit. His skin, black hair and fingernails all shone with an unnatural gloss.

"Rowan, it is so good to see you," the man said in an American accent with only the slightest Japanese inflection.

On a reflex, Rowan also latched shut the top button of his suit, leaving creases where the fabric strained against his belly.

"How are you, Mango, ya old cunt?"

The Japanese man pursed his lips and pressed his hands down in the air a few times in front of his belt, a warning out of sight of the van's occupants.

"Be careful, my man, a few of our guests speak pretty good English. Are we ready to go?"

"Yeah, no worries. But are you sure these blokes have the dollars to help me out here?"

"No problems, Rowan. This is 1986. It's the Japanese century, brother. These guys got the yen and they got the *yen*. They want to buy up half of Queensland, and I think they might do it."

Rowan couldn't hold back his smile. "What are you waiting for then? Let's do this."

Mango bounded back to the van. He bowed politely and smiled as he helped six Japanese men in black business suits, all with grey hair—either a little or a lot—climb out onto the dust. One of them had an SLR camera around his neck, the lens cap already removed.

Good thing Rowan wore his black suit today. He better not call Mango by that name in front of the others. His friend's name was really Takeo Hashimoto. "Call me Ted," Mango had suggested when Rowan first met him two years ago. Ted was nursing a bad sunburn at their first meeting, after bobbing on a boat in Moreton Bay trying to broker a shopping centre purchase between a Tokyo retail firm and a foul-breathed Brisbane property magnate who was short on cash but enjoyed drinking imported beers on his forty-six foot Peterson cutter.

"You look more like a mango to me," Rowan had told him after his fourth scotch. "Red on the outside, but yellow through and through." Luckily, Mango had laughed and was happy to let the name stick.

"Rowan, allow me to introduce our esteemed visitors from Japan," Mango said as the last of the men stepped out of the van.

Rowan thrust his hand out, and then withdrew it, bowing quickly to each man.

The tallest man, who also had the thinnest slick of hair, said something to Mango. Most of the Japanese laughed. Sensing he was the butt of the joke, Rowan laughed with them.

"Well, this is the place," Rowan announced, pausing for effect. "This is the home of the future 'Wild Lion Safari Park.'"

The shortest of the men, one of those who didn't laugh at Mango's joke, said something quietly to Mango in Japanese.

"Ah so," Mango said, and turned to Rowan. "Fukuda-san points out that, ah, the name of the park on your prospectus you sent him had both lions and tigers in the title."

Rowan hesitated. Mango looked expectantly at him.

"Oh, that. Yeah, well on scientific advice from my, uh, science experts, I found out tigers and lions don't mix that well."

Mango translated the answer for the short man, who nodded noncommittally.

"Yes," Rowan went on. "It was strictly for reasons of nature that I've chosen to keep it just lions, with also cheetahs and maybe a few leopards. We're still sourcing those animals."

Mango translated, and the men nodded, except the man with the camera, who ignored him and took photos in every direction.

The youngest man spoke quietly to Mango, smiling while he kept his eyes on Rowan's face. Mango turned to Rowan and winked.

"Okudaira-san says this is a very exciting concept, one that he is sure boys and girls from around the world would want to see."

"Thank you, sir," Rowan stammered, his heart racing faster than he wished. "I agree. This is an excellent family-themed idea."

"Your funding model—I trust a man of your experience has no doubt carefully thought through what is needed?" The man with the camera said.

"Oh, well, that's straight to the guts, isn't it," Rowan said. He cleared his throat. "Our business plan offers a two-level partnership proposal. The largest investor would own a thirty percent stake, for a modest commitment of two-point-seven million dollars."

He felt his chest widen and his back straighten as he continued.

"Mango, I mean Mister Hashimoto, can assist you with translating that into yen. The smaller investor would command fifteen percent for an outlay of a mere one-point-four million."

Mango looked strangely at Rowan, who realised he had been yelling to help them understand, then turned to the group and spoke

Japanese. Rowan thought he heard Mango say "million" a few times. He tried to read the faces of the men, all of them standing still, except for the short one with the camera, who continued taking photos.

The men nodded slowly and lowered their eyes to the ground as they listened, or stared ahead inscrutably, their lips pouting as if about to kiss one of the flies circling their shiny heads.

"What about the distance to market?" one of them asked with a British accent. Rowan turned to see a man at the end of the group, who hadn't spoken before.

"To market? You mean..." Rowan said, not sure what he meant.

"To market," the man replied. "You say in your prospectus that you plan on using the half million person population of the greater Gold Coast as your base, both tourists and residents?"

"That's projected population. We'll hit half million by 2000 for sure," Rowan replied, a sinking feeling flooding into his stomach.

"Yes, but the heart of the Gold Coast is over forty miles away, yes?"

"Yeah, maybe."

"Isn't that too far away?"

Rowan laughed nervously. "Not for us Aussies, mate. Distance is nothin'. Crikey, a honeybee flies farther than that to poop."

The men looked to Mango for translation, but he smiled fixedly at Rowan, ignoring them.

"What I mean is, maybe in Japan forty miles is a long way, but here, people like to drive here. Mostly Japanese cars these days, I might add."

A cold drop of sweat slid down Rowan's ribs.

"But you are no doubt familiar with the paper in the Cornell Hotel Administration Journal," the man continued, his British accent stiffening with each word. "It was a study at the University of Florida. Proximity is key to success for family amusement parks. According to their equation, a half million person metropolitan area would need the park to be within twenty miles of the urban border for that park to be viable. Your wildlife park would be almost twice that distance away."

Rowan smiled, waiting for the laughter from the other Japanese. But it didn't come. They tilted their heads and looked at him as if he were about to perform a song. Except for the man with the camera. He seemed fixated on the lion cut-outs under the distant clump of trees.

"Mango, you gotta tell them. This is Australia, mate. This isn't a Yank project. People will drive here, don't worry about that." Rowan swung his arms wide, indicating the stretch of shrivelled grass. "And look at all the parking."

"Scuse me, sir. Is that one breeding?" The man with the camera was pointing at the cut-outs.

"Pardon?" Rowan said.

"Is that animal breeding?"

Rowan looked at Mango. They smiled, relieved at the change of subject.

"Well, if he is breeding, we probably shouldn't be watching."

He and Mango laughed, but the other men turned to look at the cut-outs.

"No," the camera man said. "That one over there. Its stomach is red. Is it hurt?"

"Oh, you mean, is he *bleeding*?" Rowan said. "No, no, he's okay. Just must have got some paint or some dust or something on his chest."

The Japanese men talked quickly in Japanese. The camera man let a few of them view the lions through his telephoto lens.

Rowan's panic grew. "Or maybe he's just killed something."

Several of them turned to him, alarmed. They quickly translated for the others. A wave of disquiet rippled through the group. They talked animatedly. A few of them pointed at the Hiace van.

Rowan stepped toward them, causing him to wince as pain shot up his leg. "No, they don't kill people or big animals. I mean, they could, but they're perfectly safe. I mean it might have been a lizard or a snake or something."

With that, the men who could understand English started scanning the nearby grass. The men chattered quickly, one of them grabbing Mango's arm imploringly. He bowed and raised his hands to calm them, speaking reassuringly in Japanese, but they were already moving towards the Hiace. Rowan tried to block them.

"No, no, don't go. Please stay. I have food for you. Raw fish!" The men looked at Rowan oddly and walked more quickly towards the van.

"Don't go, please. We have lots to talk about." Rowan unbuttoned his jacket and wiped sweat from his forehead with his sleeve.

"Mango, tell them it's okay."

Mango opened the van door and the men piled in. He hurried over to Rowan, smiling nervously.

"What gives, Mango?" Rowan asked, his face pressed close to his friend's. "Are these blokes fair dinkum or not? This is going to be worth millions, mate. Millions!"

Rowan yelled over to the van. "Hey, bring your camera. I've got a real live lion right here in that cage!"

Mango gently grabbed Rowan's upper arms.

"Sure, that's great, mate. Look they've got a busy schedule today. I've to keep them moving or it's my ass, okay?"

"But we haven't even talked details yet."

Mango moved away to the van, smiling back at Rowan.

"Yes I know, mate. I'll call you. Tonight. I promise, I will call you at home."

"Yeah, but…" Rowan's shoulders collapsed as the door slammed shut and the van quickly circled and headed back out the driveway.

"Un-fucking-believable," Rowan muttered.

"What did they say?" Greg stood on the stairs to the site office, eating a sushi roll.

"Aw, nothing. I'll sort it out with them later."

Greg licked his fingers. "I read about this sushi stuff. It's actually pretty tasty. Where did you find it?"

Rowan ignored him and stared at the receding dust cloud stirred up by the Hiace.

Greg shifted uneasily. "You want me to take that lion back to Toowoomba straight away? The zoo bloke sounded worried about him."

"Nah, fuck him." Rowan looked over at the cage as if for the first time. "You should go home. You've done enough today."

Greg shrugged and loped over to his car.

"Don't forget to unhook the trailer," Rowan said tiredly.

"Oh, yeah."

Greg unlatched the lion's cage and swung the jack down to prop up the trailer.

"I'll see you in the morning then," Greg said.

"Huh?"

"To take the lion back. There's a bucket of cow guts in the bottom shelf of the fridge if he gets peckish."

"Yeah, all right," Rowan said.

Greg smiled uneasily, his Adam's apple riding up and down as if wanting to launch one more statement. Instead he climbed into his car and turned the ignition until his fan belt screeched.

Rowan watched the car bounce over the rock littered driveway, its dusty rear window greying the young man's blond hair, which shuddered as the car hit potholes.

The hot westerly wind sent the dust of the car's wake drifting across the scratchy weeds.

Rowan went over to the cage. The lion was awake now, its head up, following him lazily like a dog watching a falling leaf. It yawned widely, showing its rotting teeth, most worn down to dark stumps.

"Looks like it's you and me, Leo. You want to go back to that zoo now? To the one square meal a day?"

The lion locked eyes with Rowan, sensing a change in his voice. It blinked, and shook off a fly circling close to its ear.

Rowan stared hard at the lion's face, its sloping nose scuffed like an old brown carpet. "How many fights you had, mate? How many kills? How many roots did you score, eh?"

The lion fixed his stare on Rowan, who returned it before letting out a long sigh.

"I know what you need, mate." Rowan went over to the cage door. He hesitated. He sighed again. With both hands he unlatched the door. It swung open with rusty complaint.

"Come on, big fella. Time to go."

The lion didn't move.

Rowan limped over to where the lion's bulk pushed against the cage, its hair poking through gaps in the wire. He gave the cage a solid whack.

"Come on, Leo. Move your arse!"

He slapped at the cage again and the lion rose awkwardly to all fours. Rowan slapped the cage yet again.

"Move it, fuzz-face, let's go!"

The lion tilted his head and roared loudly with annoyance. Rowan took a step back, rattled. He crept to the open cage door, carefully swinging his arm in front of the open space, willing the beast to step out of the cage.

The lion took a step toward the door.

"That's it, champ. The time has come."

Its great mane rubbed against the cage opening as if scratching an itch. Rowan stepped to the side of the cage for protection.

"Go on, big fella. Jump!" he said as he gave the cage another whack.

The lion scowled, its whiskers twitching. It lifted one paw, then another, and leaped out of the cage. The vibration of one hundred and fifty kilos of carnivore impacting the ground made Rowan flinch.

The lion sniffed the air, looking around as if waiting for someone to direct it.

"Move it, mate. If you're going to cark it, you might as well do it on your terms. Go on, get out!" Rowan shouted, kicking dust at the big cat.

It lumbered away, past the site office, then stopped.

Rowan stepped out from behind the cage door and walked closer to the lion. "What are you waiting for? Go!"

The lion looked back at Rowan with wet, piercing eyes. Rowan's pounding heartbeat counted the seconds until the cat shook the dust from its mane, turned and ambled west into the towering grass. The last sight Rowan had of it was the flick of its tail high above the reeds, until it was lost in the void between the golden wall of grass and the dark line of trees sheltering Lake Wyaralong.

Rowan looked at the landscape for a long time, then turned and walked painfully back toward the office, holding his thigh for support.

What to tell that tightwad zookeeper in Toowoomba? "Aw, bugger him," he said out loud. "'The miserable beast dropped dead from the excitement of getting out of your jail'—that's what I'll tell the bastard." He chuckled to himself. His throat caught and he hacked several times.

A wall of cold air poured over him when he opened the office door. He slowly climbed the stairs and went over to his desk, leaving the door open behind him.

He dialled the phone and waited, his breath wheezing from exertion. His chin held the phone to his shoulder as he patted his pockets till he found his cigarettes. He slid one into his lips.

"Yes, hi, it's me," he said into the phone.

He paused, listening.

"Nah, no good. The Japs are all talk. Mango took me for a ride this time."

He listened and nodded. His eyes drifted out the window to the dark streak of forest stretched to the west.

"Yeah, I should be back by about four. No worries, love. I'll pick up some chocolate macadamias for you. See you then."

He put the phone back in its cradle and bent down to open the bar fridge. He pulled out a plate overflowing with sushi rolls, paused, then put it back in. "Raw tuna eatin' bastards," he muttered, then flicked off the air conditioner.

At the door he surveyed the shimmering landscape. The distant cut-outs of the lions danced in the hot torrent of air. They twirled like dervishes, except the one with the red chest. It whipped and cartwheeled with distorted, pointed limbs. Like a Scarlet Starlet.

He smiled crookedly to himself, braced his hand onto his thigh and stepped down into the brilliant sunlight.

THREE WISHES

David Stringer

Big Harry had seen a lot of things in his life: the red hills turning purple in the sunset, Annie dying of cancer and even a UFO, but nothing compared to the angel who suddenly appeared on Ferry Road. Big Harry was, I came to discover, a man full of surprises. For one thing his angel was male, with a cheeky smile and a knowing wink...but all of that came later. At first Deva, (for that apparently was his name), simply appeared as a bright white light hovering about the height of the street sign....

"A bit like that time I saw a UFO," he smiled slightly and turned to gauge my reaction on the first night I met him at the hospital.

Seeing my interest he continued. "Out back on the farm one night, years ago it was. At first I thought it was a meteor but it didn't burn out, simply kept on heading towards the hills, zigged and zagged a couple of times then just faded away."

I couldn't help asking, "Do you believe in aliens then?"

"God no," he chuckled. Then his big face settled into seriousness. "But I know what I saw."

And so he did.

There was a refreshing honesty and simplicity to Big Harry which I put down to his being a man of the land. Hundreds of storms and sunsets, birthing lambs and butchering stock had honed his heart to an acceptance of both the ugliness and the beauty of life and death. All those fantasies which city men spin around themselves just deflate and blow away in the face of the land's vast and quiet awareness. He had been a rugby man too once, quite a promising one I'd heard, and you soon learn in the depths of a ruck when the first knee or elbow crunches into your face, that bullshit talks but the truth walks. So I got interested when Harry began telling me his story of Deva.

Harry had been finding his way by counting the streets as he always did, right into the heart of the menacing darkness of that part of town where I work—and where we had kind of found each other in the weeks after Annie died. By all accounts she was a tough, straight-talking woman who had been beside him through all the years of hardship, when the red dust seemed to choke the very cracks of their skin and even the crows were too dry to caw. And when in some kind of sad symbolic metaphor they found Annie was as barren as the land they clung to, he never once used it against her.

And then came the cancer. They found it too late of course, for she wasn't a doctor-botherer, and in the blink of an eye their life together on the land was rooted up and left to die like a mangled stump in the sun; and their new life was hospital rooms and cold steel machines that swallowed her frail body to record the advance of unstoppable death. He was out walking the night she passed, when she released into the arms of her God like a puff of dust in the breeze, and he wasn't there to hold those frail little hands, which he had done all day every day for the last few months of her life.

"They'd done beautiful things, those hands." He didn't look at me, just stared straight ahead, and I wondered if there were tears he didn't want me to see. "Wiped the sweat from my face for two weeks straight when I caught the river fever... even milked her cow.'" He fell silent a few moments recalling her gentleness. "Heidi." I must have raised an eyebrow so he explained, "Her pet cow, Heidi. Not for the freezer, that one.... And all that painting she would do—Japanese stuff, with a brush and ink, those funny letters, you know? She was so fond of doing anything Japanese...." He sighed and settled his eyes away into the distance.

And so he returned every night by counting the streets, perhaps in his own way hoping to find her here once more; which is where I would always find him and gradually he told me his story. He was writing it too. He showed me all the scraps of paper he kept in his pocket because he felt it was something he wanted to share with people. He'd sit and write there at the little table in our lunchroom, such a big man all hunched up awkwardly, concentrating so intently on his mission before they came to take him back...but that couldn't go on forever of course. Nothing does.

He first saw Deva on Ferry Road, as I said. It was the night Annie passed and Deva had come to let him know, so he could hurry back and be there in time to touch her while she was still warm; before the Earth takes back even the heat She temporarily loans us. The next time he saw Deva, so he related to me over a late night cup of Milo, was about a week later. He'd been feeling a bit low, and lonely, living in a boarding-house for elderly gents in a particularly grey area of

Southport. It seems he and Annie had virtually walked off the land which had come to belong to a big bank in Brissie, where men who used moisturizers and perfume liked to snigger at the men with faces burned by the sun into a landscape of cancers.

Deva's face was more visible this time, and Harry could make out that he was male and sported a cheeky smile.

"He told me I could have any wish granted—anything, provided it didn't change people's 'karma' too much, whatever that is." He nodded to himself, recalling the moment. "Said I'd earned it for being so kind and patient with Annie all those years."

"So what did you ask for?"

"A hooker."

I guess I don't need to tell you I did a double-take and kind of spluttered, "A hooker?"

He turned to look squarely at me and chuckled a little. "Well no… it turned out that way, but originally I just wanted a young woman."

Well I did warn you that Harry was full of surprises.

"You see," he continued, "I'd been kind of alone, shall we say, for quite a few years. Annie didn't see a need for sex if we couldn't have children, so…."

And I began to sense then the depths of quiet tragedy that underpin the lives of most of us, like that great big piece of an iceberg you never see. So all I could do was nod and he carried on.

"I feel embarrassed about it now." He avoided looking at me and I noticed how he clenched and unclenched his big gnarly hands. "I guess he caught me by surprise a bit, you know."

I couldn't help but laugh. "Well, it's not every day you see an angel, mate. I'd have been surprised too."

He let out a long sigh, "Yeah…maybe I was just being a smartarse, I dunno. But anyway, I asked to have a beautiful young female, for company like. Just once. Before I give up the ghost like poor Annie.

God bless her."

I nodded. "Fair enough. I'd probably ask for the same, given any wish. Couldn't you have asked for a few more wishes?"

He chuckled, a rumbling chuckle that boomed in his big chest. "Nearly came to that too, mate. But it's a long story and I'll tell you."

And with that I made us another Milo and he continued.

"Well Deva, you know, he just gimme a knowing smile and disappeared like, so I thought I'd upset him, but not three or four minutes later this gorgeous young thing appears out of the blue and starts talking to me."

Now I can't recall how many nights it took for Harry to recount it all to me, maybe three or four, but it got to the point where I was just hoping for one more meeting, one more chance to hear his story. Eventually I did, and as Fate would have it, he finished it on the very night they came for the final time to take him back. He knew, I think, that it would be our last talk, and I won't ever forget the glance he gave me from the back seat as they drove away into the night.

Her name was Maddy, she was all legs and blonde curls and she had an apartment nearby. From the beginning nothing really felt right—it was just too different from all that he had ever known. Like he was being dragged into an alien world, a world of the young, the female, the tech-savvy city dweller. She burned patchouli incense in her apartment and took incessant calls and texts on her iPhone, and Harry had to duck under a clothesline of drying underwear on his way to the toilet. His discomfort was only to get worse. When Maddy insisted on a condom and suggested she put it on for him, he suddenly realized the, shall we say, nitty-gritty of just what he had got into and declined her offer. To complete the dismal failure Maddy even began to give him the bum's rush as she had another client booked in and due to appear at any time. So he paid her the money she asked for and stumbled outside to make his way back home.

Well Harry thought that would be the end of the matter, but he felt so bad he went back a couple of times looking for Maddy, to apologise. Instead, he said, he found Deva.

"I was pretty shocked, I can tell you. I says to him, mate, that didn't go too well."

As you do when you're chatting with an angel; God, he cracked me up. "What did he say to that?"

"Well he never stopped bloody grinning, the bugger. He says, 'You can have another wish then, seeing as how that one came a bit unstuck.' That threw me, I can tell you."

The old sod was a natural story-teller and knew just when to let me hang there. I urged him on. "So? What did you ask for next?"

He turned and looked at me as if I'd asked a silly question. "Why, I asked if I could help young Maddy. Help her to live a good life. I realized I'd been selfish, wasted my wish." He let out a long sigh, shook his head slowly, so I figured maybe this didn't turn out too well either.

Deva apparently disappeared as usual and next thing Maddy walks up in thigh-high leather boots and a short skirt despite the chill in the air.

"If her skirt had been any shorter mate, she'd of had to powder more cheeks." He chuckled, more to himself than to me.

Of course she misunderstood his approach and figured he wanted to try for a repeat. "Hey Pops", she stroked his arm. "Did you get some Viagra over the net then?" Which he found pretty incomprehensible; he just wanted to talk to her about turning her life around. Had she thought about going to university? Which made her laugh apparently.

"Pops, half the girls at varsity are turning tricks like me to pay their frigging fees. I should know, they're undercutting me the shameless bitches."

And things went downhill from there, as they probably just had to. Her boyfriend drove past to check on her progress for the night and wasn't impressed with some old guy trying to reform his source of income. I suspect Harry's size might have scared the youth enough so that there wasn't any violence, but he'd been shaken by his brief contact with a world of such callous greed and degradation. And he felt bad that he had rubbed against that world and some of its filth had clung to him, yet he hadn't been able to rub some goodness off back. He lurched off into the darkness with her words ringing in his ears: "What gives you the right to criticize my life, grandpa? You sure wanted a part of it the other night.'" And together with her pimp they shouted obscenities after him as he hurried away.

I'm sure that was the night we found him wandering around where the blue flashing police lights bounce off the brick walls and car yard signs. By this time we were getting concerned about him and were keeping an eye out as we drove the ambulance near the hospital. I remember he seemed particularly upset that night—didn't utter a word, which was unlike him.

He thought he'd never see Deva again, but he was wrong. For this one last visit he appeared in Harry's bedroom in the home for elderly gents; this time he was a little more serious.

"So what did you learn Harry, from those two wishes—anything?"

"Well, I learned not to poke my nose into other people's lives."

Deva nodded. "People have to sort out their own karma, Harry. You can't do it for them, as you just become a part of it. And what of the first wish?"

"I learned I hadn't really missed anything great all these years. I thought I missed sex, but when you see it just plain, just as it is—there's nothing much to miss."

"That's a couple of great lessons, Harry. Tell me, what do you think now you should have wished for?"

"That's easy," he replied without hesitation. "I guess it's too late now, but I really wish I could just see Annie—one more time."

Apparently Deva just stared at him, quietly and for quite a long time, before he smiled and disappeared. But this wasn't like the other times. This time Harry seemed to be rushing headlong down a tunnel of light to find himself sitting in a room, a room he had never seen before—one he could barely even imagine. It was light and airy, with walls made of fine paper and exquisite wood, some with paintings on them, and slowly he began to recognize it as Japanese. He had seen pictures in Annie's books and magazines, and even in her paintings. He became aware of someone else in the room and saw a young woman about 20 years old standing at an easel, brushes in hand. She had the pretty features, fair skin and jet black hair of a Japanese girl and wore a turquoise gold-embroidered kimono. She smiled, and he knew immediately that it was Annie.

"How did you come here?" she asked, so he explained Deva and the wish. "That's so sweet—but you can't stay, Harry."

"How come you're so young?" he asked.

"Time is different here. Don't ask. It's just—different."

"You're Japanese now?"

She smiled. "Sort of. But this is not Earth—so maybe it's not Japanese. You must go back, Harry. You can't stay here."

"But I want to be with you, Annie—forever."

She came to him and touched a finger gently to his lips. "What you once knew as Annie has gone, Harry. Gone back to the Earth. You have to let go." He began to cry and she wiped away his tears. "Come on, let's sit outside for a bit," and she led him out to where he could see beautiful gardens and a huge pond full of water-lilies of all colours. They sat for a while on a stone bench and she held his hand. Eventually he asked, "If the Annie I knew has gone...then who are you?"

After thinking about it she replied, "I'm just everything that Annie ever wanted Harry… and ever didn't want. Her hopes, her dreams, her fears. We arise and we pass, like a wave in the ocean. You must learn to let go, Harry." She squeezed his hand and looked away into the distance, across the water. "Harry, do you remember that big old wooden gate? At the end of our farm road, opening into our lovely gardens?"

He was perplexed, but nodded, remembering it well. She continued.

"And do you remember, my love, both the coming and the going?" She looked directly at him, her young eyes full of love and caring. And suddenly, in a dizzying rush, he understood.

She stood up and bent to kiss him, to kiss his sun-ravaged scalp, and helped him to his feet where he towered over her tiny form.

"It's time, my love."

He nodded and followed her back into the room. Deva was waiting to guide him back and he was once more in his dingy bedroom at the boarding-house. He couldn't stay there—just couldn't. So he did what he did most nights and went out walking. And like most nights he ended up at the hospital with me. Only this would be the last time because the authorities had become concerned for his safety and he was being placed under 'care'. Dementia, they called it. Senile dementia. No-one warns you when you come into this world, all bright-eyed and bushy-tailed, that the exit is often ignominious and painful. Or maybe they do but you just don't want to look.

I think he knew who they were and where they were taking him, because he came to me and shook my hand, thanked me for the nights of Milo and a willing ear. As he turned to go I just had to ask:

"What *was* it about that gate? What was the *coming* and the *going*?"

He stopped in his tracks, seemed to look right through me— perhaps seeing Annie one more time, as she was.

"When we got married and I took her home to the farm, I carried her through that gate. We were young and full of dreams, so I swept her off her feet and carried her into the garden around our house." By now the nurses were drawing closer and I swear I saw him shudder. "That was the coming. Then when we had to walk off the land because we couldn't repay the bank, I had to carry her again—to the car. She was so sick you see. Couldn't walk. We said goodbye then to everything we loved." He sighed. "That was the going."

And with that he turned and was escorted to the waiting vehicle; he gave me that last knowing glance and was gone, into another life. I walked slowly into the lunchroom, and as I sat down I saw all the torn up scraps of paper, the story he'd been writing, thrown into the rubbish bin. He'd let it all go, you see—as we all must do one day. It's just our coming and our going.

THE CLEARING

Di Morris

Margaret

I found myself ringing the Trelaurel Forest Lodge three weeks after Hugh died. It was a quiet death, and a dignified one. Always the gentleman, Hugh asked me would I be all right after he went. I said, "Yes," even though my heart was screaming no. He closed his eyes, took three more breaths, and left me forever.

We met because of Trelaurel. We were both amateur photographers from a city club which I joined a few months after I got my first secretarial job. I bought a Pentax single lens reflex camera and signed up for a weekend in the rainforest. It was a way of establishing some independence even though I still lived at home with my mother.

We travelled by bus, and I found myself sitting with Hugh. He was much older than I, and he inspired confidence. During the two hour journey he taught me most of what I needed to know about my new camera. He was kind, educated (he wrote poetry and had his own portrait photography business), and a very good teacher. Six months later, after many such weekends, I agreed to become engaged and a year after that we were married quietly in a registry office. In that eighteen months leading up to my wedding day I experienced strange, strong physical feelings when he held me, but I was brought up to believe that the bride should save herself for marriage. I looked forward to our first night as man and wife with great anticipation.

We honeymooned at Trelaurel, of course. Our bedroom faced a panorama of mountains, so even after that night of horrid revelation the morning sun spreading like a soft gold cloth over the peaks still filled us with pleasure.

Hugh enfolded me in his arms and said, "Don't worry about it, dear. It will sort itself out."

It never did.

We threw ourselves into a week of walking—rain or sun. I took some of my best photographs ever during that time. I took pictures of sunlight streaming in crepuscular rays through a dense canopy, buttressed roots clasping the forest floor, a wompoo pigeon framed by a thicket of green. It was as if I had put all my passion into capturing the essence of the forest.

Dear Hugh smiled despite everything.

We tried again sometimes, but it seemed like a chore by then. Finally we embraced our celibate life with relief. I loved Hugh like a father and a brother—neither of which I'd ever had, being an only child whose mother was widowed when I was three.

I began doing the secretarial work for his office. Then, as I learned more, I became a partner. People said we were like twins in the end, despite the age difference. Often we could finish each other's sentences.

Now it is as though half of me died along with Hugh and the living half is slowly being starved of vital elements. So I have come back for the last time to Trelaurel and the rainforest.

All beginnings must have an end.

Tracey

Jesus, I was thinking when I got here, what sort of effing place is this? The way Fabio talked it was going to be like a kind of health farm situation—massages, spa pools, yoga and all that. But it looked like some sort of back woods place full of hiking types. I wasn't sure if little brother Rocky's birthday present was a joke or not, but Fabio had loved it. Good thing that business problem came up at the last minute and he couldn't make it, or he would've played merry hell with the management. Fabio likes to get his way. And his massages.

He can't stand the thought of wasting money, even if it was a special and a present. He said I should go check it out anyway, and it would be good for my education.

"These places got class—you know?" he said.

It's not enough for him that I look like a million dollars when I scrub up, he wants me to act like I grew up in effing Vaucluse and went to a private school.

I'm surprised he didn't give his half of the present to his mother—but knowing me, something about ol' Fabio boy's shady activities was bound to slip out. And he wouldn't like that. Mama thinks the sun shines out of his rear-end; never asks where the money comes from to keep her in her dinky little Rose Bay apartment.

It was just before lunch when I arrived. I think I was slightly pissed but the driver helped me down the steps. Thank god he caught me before I broke the heel of the new Pradas on that stupid crazy paving. Fabio bought them for me, and there'll be hell to pay if I show up again without them.

Some of the clients have requirements about footwear, the more expensive the better.

Margaret

Our beloved Trelaurel has changed. I am shocked to see people here who might just as well have spent their holiday at a Club Med, or whatever they call it. Hugh would have smiled and pronounced some quote about the world changing. But I am affronted. It offends all my memories of times when everyone up here was like-minded, similarly dressed in sensible walking kit, with strong shoes and cheerful faces. It was a balm to be amongst such folk.

I have just seen a woman get off the bus wearing extremely high heels. Not only that, but a low cut dress and thick gold jewellry that would be more suitable for a racecourse. Naturally, she did not balance very well on such unsuitable footwear. In fact, if the driver had not taken her arm as she alighted I think she would have fallen. Did no-one tell her that she would not need makeup and town clothes? She also said something vulgar as she stumbled; a dreadful word that my mother would have washed out of my mouth with soap and water, had I ever uttered it. I turned my head away.

Now that I am here I eat, I walk, I tend to my shoes because Hugh taught me that was the most important thing to do in the rainforest. But a hollowness eats at me. I feel alienated and alone, though people speak to me kindly.

There is only one person who engenders any warmth in me. He

is young, very handsome, and also alone. But he smiles. He dresses sensibly, and I noted that his shoes were absolutely right for bushwalking.

Adam

I only had that corny ad for Trelaurel Mountain Lodge on the highway billboard to go by when I applied for the job, but I liked the look of the mountains behind the girl and guy toasting each other with bubbly on a balcony at sunset. The trees looked like wool they were so thick. It reminded me of this story Mum tells about me.

We were camping in a National Park when I was four. I wandered off and got lost for an hour. Mum says she and Dad nearly went crazy before they found me. But the worst thing happened a few days later. Apparently I said something like, "I want to be lost in the forest again." That *really* freaked her out. Camping trips of any sort were off the holiday list from then on.

Anyway, Trelaurel took me on. And so far it's pretty good—a complete change from Uni which was getting so stressful it was doing my head in. My room is in the staff quarters with the cleaners and cook and I've been told to familiarise myself with the place so I can lead guided walks and generally make myself useful when they need another hand maintaining the tracks.

The first morning I forced myself to get out of bed and take a five kilometre hike with the guidebook before breakfast. Wearing those green trousers and shirt they gave me I must have blended in with the scenery because none of the scrub turkeys or pademelons gave me a second look. Dad's old waterproof boots and the thick wool socks Mum bought me came in handy when I had to cross a few rocky creek beds. Slowly, all the stuff I ever knew about rainforests started coming back to me. The wind got up in the canopy, and I felt great.

It was pure luck that I found the clearing. There seemed to be a change in the light so I went in off the track a hundred yards or so and found out why. Man, it was something, the way one giant fallen tree opened up that forest. Light poured down on me as I stood there taking it all in and wondering whether I would keep my discovery to myself. I've always been a bit of a loner, but this time it made sense. From now on this place would be the site of an awesome battle as every sapling strained to make it to the canopy first. Trampling feet would wreck everything nature was trying to do.

Later, back in the dining room I was working my way through a stack of eggs, bacon and sausages when I noticed this woman a bit older than my mother staring at me. She was wearing the sort of khaki gear they had in that old movie *Out of Africa*. When I got up for more toast she seemed to be looking hard at my shoes. I couldn't help smiling because she reminded me of a possum with her googly eyes and little round glasses. It didn't matter that she saw this, because she gave me a sort of smile back.

Tracey

It's so bloody boring here. And it's cold. Or maybe it's just the alcohol and nicotine deprivation that Fabio made me swear to on the Bible. So far I've kept it up.

One of the rooms had a big log fire burning all day. Fabio would've gone nuts over it. He thinks that's the ultimate in class. I was just glad to have somewhere warm. And you can't call sitting next to a fire and breathing in fumes actually smoking. But it helped.

What didn't help was the rainforest kid and that stupid prissy woman in her brown gear gawking at me whenever they went past.

They think I didn't see, but what they don't know is I've got a built-in radar for being watched. Fabio says it's a gift—sorts your potential clients out quick smart.

I got a book about rainforests off the shelf. Fabio expects me to be a bloody expert when this is over. Says it sounds good if you can talk the talk, wants me to take it all back to him—that 's another way of getting his money's worth. But I didn't even look at it. I dozed all day in front of a fire like an effing grandma. Grandma Tracey! The rest of the girls'll laugh when I tell them that one. I'm dying for a good laugh—better than a fix any day.

Adam

When there's a fire burning in the lounge there's a good strong spice smell coming off the beams. A woman sat by it all day yesterday. She was breathing deeply and staring into the flames. Maybe she was stoned. Anyway, she stayed there all day curled up like a cat. She had a book but she didn't pick it up when I was looking.

She was drunk or high when she got here, and I swear she was dressed for shopping—like a hijack from a Pacific Fair boutique or something. Her hair was long and blonde and puffed out and her face was plastered with gunk—all round her eyes mainly. She must be thirty-five at least.

Possum woman nearly had a fit when this one arrived. She adjusted her glasses, and almost lifted one side of her lip the way animals do when they're going to growl, but she was either too polite or couldn't be bothered.

With cat woman, it's like they brought an exotic animal to an Australian Zoo and she's having her settling in period. It'll be interesting to see what she does when she finally snaps out of it.

Margaret

The time had come. I put Hugh's camera and binoculars in the rucksack along with his walking boots, and carried his walking stick. All week I had been preparing myself for this. I took water, just enough for the journey.

I had requested a very early breakfast of prunes, savoury mince on toast, and tea. I brushed my teeth, tidied my room, tied my shoelaces again and set off on the long trek, carrying Hugh's walking stick. I felt the familiar immediate drop in temperature as I entered the shade of the forest. Every sound and sight I passed seemed heightened—every leaf tremor, every bird song, every shade of dun, green and black on the forest floor. My perception was so clear that I believe I heard the call of the Albert Lyrebird—the shyest denizen of the forest.

I knew Hugh was with me in spirit. I could have vowed that he was also walking steadily along. Twice I stopped to look behind me, the feeling was so strong. I hoped I had his approval for what I intended to do.

Adam

I knew she was going to come over and talk to me. Just like possum woman, she'd started to look at me. I was eating lemon delicious and custard that night when she suddenly stood over me and said, "So, d'ya know any really good places round here?"

I swallowed a big mouthful. She repeated the question, adding, "A really special place—somewhere you could write home about…"

Her eyes were blue-green with a dark ring around the edge. I was thinking of this as I said, "I believe I do."

"My time's running out," she said. "I don't wanna fly back to

Sydney without information." Her voice reminded me of gangster movies. I had to smile.

"You'll have to get up early—that's the best time," I said.

"Sweet," she said.

So much for keeping a secret. I always was a sucker for blue-green eyes.

Margaret

It was a long walk, and not an easy one. I took a little-used turning that was a short cut to my destination over a high dangerous ridge of crumbling clay and stringy eucalypts, then down again along an old cow track which descended through cleared grassland and eventually joined the path of a stream.

Another half-hour of squelching and stumbling along this trail and I had arrived at the top of another valley, overlooking the thick forest below, standing beside an outcrop of rocks over which the water gushed and tumbled a hundred feet to more rocks below.

Nothing had changed. It was the place where Hugh and I had spent many an idyllic hour on our honeymoon. No-one ever came here, we discovered, which made the arduous trek doubly worth it. We would eat our packed lunch, beef and pickle sandwiches, an apple and a flask of tea, as though it were a royal repast, listening to the waterfall and training our binoculars in a desultory fashion over the steep slope of the valley beyond.

I put down the rucksack and squatted down to compose myself. I took out Hugh's binoculars for the last time, training the sights on the forest canopy. Suddenly I focused the lenses more closely. I could hardly believe what I was seeing in a clearing below.

Adam

We left at five-thirty. It was still dark and the cold seemed to hang about in the air, ready to give way when the light came. I like that time. She was ready when I knocked on her door. She was a strange looking bushwalker in her short shorts and a little leather jacket that left her middle bare, but at least she had socks and runners on, even if they looked too expensive for getting muddy.

I had hoped she wasn't a talker. But she opened up and started questioning me straight away. What was this tree, what made that hole, why are the leaves red—that sort of thing.

"Don't you know?" I said.

"I never been outside Sydney since I got there," she said. "Not even to the Blue Mountains."

"Why not?" I asked.

"Always working," she said. She wouldn't say more.

So I told her what she wanted to know. She grabbed my arm going over a slippery rock and her hand seemed to stay there for the rest of the walk.

Maybe it was the forest. Maybe it was the early light or the time of day. Whatever it was, after a while it felt as though we were the only two people in the world.

When we got to the clearing she swore.

"Sweet effing Jesus this is like church!"

All the leaves dripped with moisture and the early sunlight turned the droplets on like lights. This time I noticed there was a waterfall not far away dropping about thirty metres down a cliff.

Wild raspberries had taken over some of the ground. I picked one.

"Here—try this."

She took it between her teeth then tasted it with the tip of her little pink tongue, still holding onto my arm. She ate it slowly, looking round up at the treetops in the direction of the waterfall. She seemed to be chewing a while, looking up there. Then she spat out a seed, and her voice changed to husky as she grinned back at me. It made my skin prickle.

"How old are you anyway?"

"Twenty. Why?"

"C'mere."

It came right out of the blue, just like that.

We unzipped ourselves, not in such a hurry, but still hungry, and she lay down on her little leather jacket amongst the leaves. It wasn't like the movies either—more like squealing grunting pigs. I don't know where the sounds came from, her or me, maybe both.

The birds called and the wind drifted over us, afterwards. Nothing had changed. But then she started to laugh and laugh.

Apart from the laughing, which was freaky, it was great. I stroked her cat hair. It felt rough, but nice. I could have gone again, but she got up quickly.

Margaret

The size of it was most shocking. He was only a young man but it rose up in the morning sunlight like a shaft. Hugh had never achieved more than a mild tumescence. My eyes were glued to the binoculars, and I felt myself to be gasping for air. There was a discomfort in my lower abdomen that shifted lower then fluttered into a stream of sensations down my leg as I watched her open her legs to receive him. As he began to pump at her, the binoculars fell from my hands, my legs squeezed together involuntarily and my body seemed to implode with a melting sensation.

After the internal pulsing ceased, it took me minutes to recover my senses as I sat by the tree where Hugh and I had pledged our sweet, barren lives to each other. I knew what I had experienced, for I had purchased many books on the subject of married life in an effort to help Hugh.

With the waterfall chuckling in my ears and the early sunlight caressing me with the benison of its warmth, I realised that I was not ashamed of my body's involuntary reaction to the union that took place down in the clearing between those two young people. I fancy she was the instigator, but it was evident that he quickly responded.

Hugh and I had often watched bird and animal mating rituals with great interest through our binoculars. I was never in the least repulsed by the urges of nature.

Rather, it was that glimpse of the reality of human life in the wild that jolted me into the present and into the world of my own needs. It was as though I had been catapulted through a barrier into another part of a world I thought I knew, but which I had never really experienced properly before.

Adam

She didn't want to stay long in the clearing. We made good time on the way back with her in the lead, stopping only when there was a fork in the track to ask the way. I got the feeling she was thinking hard, but not about me. But it was all okay that we would probably never see each other again.

What happened back there was a bit like having a drink of water when you're thirsty. After the drink you forget about it. Some guys would want to tell the world—or at least boast to their mates. I could even see the heading in a trashy True-Life magazine: I Had a Blast With a Hot Mystery Chick in the Middle of the Rainforest type of thing. But it wasn't like that for me. More like a warm feeling inside. My secret.

We got back to the Lodge just before the dining room closed. The cook was a bit annoyed, but he put all the leftovers of sausage and bacon and beans on a big plate and left us to it. Now that I was back I wanted to ask her my questions—where do you live, what do you do, what's your ambition and all that. The way people do. And also how old she was exactly.

But she had gone off into her other world of wherever she came from.

"Sorry I can't stay—got to catch the bus," she said, after one bite of sausage. "Look after yourself. Don't do anything I wouldn't do." She messed my hair a bit and winked, then she was gone.

Margaret

What had I really thought the ceremonial throwing over the falls of Hugh's bushwalking paraphernalia would achieve? I envisaged with shame the possibility of some poor bush creature being startled or even injured by those missiles crashing through the water and bouncing off the rocks.

Afterwards, I even laughed a little at the notion as I carried the heavy rucksack all the way back to the Lodge. It also would have been such a waste! The camera was slightly heavier than recent models of the same make, but still one of the best money could buy. Hugh's binoculars were his particular pride and joy. Had we a son, they would have gone to him.

The next day I left both at the desk, requesting they be given to that nice young man, Adam, whose place in my memory will ever be linked with leaf and forest and sunlit glades of youthful exuberance.

I wrote him a note wishing him a happy life, and quoted Horace's Carpe Diem. I wonder if he will understand. No matter.

I am now bursting with long suppressed ideas for ways a small company just might modernise portrait photography. And I will join another society where people of like mind meet and mingle. I am still of an age to do so.

Tracey

Fabio was right, mountain air does you a power of good. But not in the way he figured. I'm still young—and I plan to enjoy my life the way I want. I'm taking up smoking again, I'm going to drink what I like, say what I like, shag who I like, do what I want. I don't care if I die at forty so long as I've lived up till then. And he can take it or leave it. Come to think of it, I won't be too pissed if he leaves it.

And when I think of that kooky old girl up there with her binoculars, and what she saw, I want to crack up all over again. I always did like practical jokes, but this was one of my best.

The old Tracey is back! Lucky for me the kid was obliging. He didn't know—probably thought he just got lucky. All in a day's work for me, but that time I got laughs out of it instead of bucks. That's what made the difference—the laughs. Once I started I couldn't stop. I never want to stop.

Funny though, I reckon the kid in the rainforest was the only guy I've ever known who wanted nothing. That made me think, too.

No—it's Tracey time now, and I'm getting the hell out of here and living it up on the Gold Coast for a while. And if I run out of money, well, making some more won't be too hard with my experience, thanks to good ol' Fabio.

Adam

Everything has settled down since they left. Maybe it was just my imagination that it all seemed so weird at first. Possum woman turned out to be really nice—she left me a camera and her husband's binoculars that must be worth a fair bit of money because I've tried them out and they're really powerful and clear.

I asked the receptionist to forward the letter I wrote thanking her and telling her about the Albert Lyrebird I've seen. No doubt about it, people change for the better up here. It's two months since I came and I've seen them arrive full of complaints and demands, but before they leave they're a friend.

I found out cat woman's name. Therese Wilkins. She cut short her stay here and Bert the bus driver told me he dropped her off at Versace. He reckons she's a tart if ever he saw one. Whatever. All I know is, in the forest she was crazy impulsive, but still okay.

That's what I love most about the forest—it's like a great leveller. Nobody can keep up pretences with all that wilderness around them. I've deferred study for a year, maybe more, or even forever. There's a lot to learn up here. The way I see it now, something that was over-towering in my life has taken a fall and I want to see what grows up in the clearing.

FRANGIPANIS

Kathleen Bleakley

Hibiscus, always the first colours—hot pink and yellow on arriving. The airport air thick. Sticky car trip past the never ending and forever revolving high rise. Dad orating about the new ones. The new shopping malls. His eyes wandering from the road. He won't hear of me taking a taxi.

Then the canals. I breathe in the space. Welcome retreat from it all. Dad makes us a cuppa tea. Strong like he and Mum drank it, and just how I like it. He passes a plate of Saos with slabs of cheddar. Airline food still in my belly, I accept one. He's made them specially for me.

I wake with light streaming in. Dad snoring from down the hall. Head for the beach. Run up to Nobby Beach. The enormous slide at

Magic Mountain. We loved it on holidays. I wore that grin—the one I've got in the photo—often.

That photo of us three at Currumbin is my favourite. Lorikeets on our heads and in our hands. Little Pete looking down. Maybe a bit scared or just camera shy. Mum was always snapping up those moments. Filling family albums with us at the beach, eating dripping ice creams and burying each other.

Amongst the parrots, Phil looking into somewhere beyond where we littlies were at. A slight frown. Think he knew before we did that Mum was sick. We probably knew too but she was full of energy. Like a pup leaping into the waves, splashing us and Dad.

I throw myself under a wave. Catch my breath—still spring. Hot by standards down south but the water hasn't warmed up yet. I run back. Dad has made a pot of tea. Head in the papers. Looks up "It's good to have you here love." I know it's hard for him. Now just sharing the mornings with the birds in the garden, the water dragons on the back fence.

Anniversaries—we don't name them but know that I come at the same time every year. Sometimes Pete or Phil join us. It's harder for them to get away. Both with kids and busy jobs: Phil a lawyer, and Pete a nurse. Pete, loved by the oldies, stopping to chat on his rounds. His shy smile making the day for someone who won't get a visitor till the weekend or even Christmas.

When Mum went to the hospice we visited most days. Played cards with her, when she was well enough to sit up. Read stories we'd written. She smiled a lot and said a little. Showed drawings we'd done for her. I know she loved my one of the parrots. All colour, big beaks & feathers.

I picked frangipanis, heady and sweet. The pinky ones, Mum's favourite, by her bedside in the last hours. Now Dad and I walk the paths covered in frangipani petals. Scatter them on her stone. Sitting on her bench in the late afternoon sun, with the rainbow lorikeets flying by.

THAT GIRL
NO MORE

Britt Melville

My first brush with drowning took place in a cardboard box. We'd rolled into the beach car park at Port Macquarie in our blue Kingswood just an hour before, spewing kids, cricket bats and beach umbrellas out of the long backseat and onto the sand nearby. It was the start of an exotic beach holiday, three hours and a whole lifetime away from our home in Sydney's southern suburbs—or 'The Shire' as it's known.

My brothers, like a pair of mini Chappell brothers, ran down the beach to set up the wickets. Naked chests, already well-tanned from afternoons playing outdoors, absorbed the glare of the early summer sun. With their sun-bleached hair and slim brown legs sticking out of scoop-sided shorts, they took turns to bowl underarm to Dad, crowing "Howzat?" after every second ball. As they fought over wickets and whose turn it was to bat, my mum and sister looked on, adjusting the straps of their crochet bikinis, making the most of the day in the sun.

Just left of the action sat a small cardboard box. While the outside proclaimed its contents to be red delicious apples, my pink gingham hat gave me away. From my makeshift playpen on the sand, I could see my brothers and dad; my mum and sister: all that was right and good in my world.

The cool, tickling fingers of the incoming tide felt nice at first. I giggled as it gently collected my box and swept me up the beach, towards the dunes. Buoyed by a second wave, I changed direction and began to pick up speed. While Mum scrambled to rescue towels and picnic baskets ambushed by the wave, I slipped away unnoticed; my red delicious cardboard ship heading swiftly—silently—out to sea. Water gushed in from holes along the side, like portholes of the *Titanic*, flooding in to cover my fat thighs. Oblivious until now of the unfolding drama, I began to cry.

Mum let out a scream.

"The baby! Quick! Somebody get the baby!"

Dad looked up from his position at the crease, his eyes following the direction of her outstretched arm, until he spotted me, bobbing amidst the waves. Characteristically unhurried, he loped across the sand and into the water to where I'd set a course for sea.

"Whoa! Where do you think you're going, Gidget?" He laughed, bending down to scoop me up, just as the next wave caught my box, flipping it up and over.

"You couldn't move quickly if you're bum was on fire!" Spat Mum, arriving seconds later to take me in her arms. Her face pale and frightened; mine red and indignant.

Dad shrugged it off. "She's all right now."

Soothed, and freed from my cardboard constraints, I wriggled in her arms, keen to return to solid ground. Mum set me down on the dry sand and I crawled off, bare bottomed, in the direction of the others, while my pink gingham hat swirled its way out to sea.

In spite of this near miss, I didn't hold a grudge against the sea. I thought that, as long as my dad was around, everything would be okay. And it was—for a while, anyway.

I learned to bodysurf when I was eight. By now, we'd moved to Queensland and, after years of either sweltering in Brisbane's western suburbs or bombing down the New England highway (in the now-upgraded Kingswood) to see the family in Sydney, someone had the bright idea to spend Christmas at Surfers Paradise.

Mum's side of the family took up position at Northcliffe, a bit away from the tourists gathered further up the strip. (We didn't consider ourselves 'tourists'. Even in those days 'tourists' came from Victoria.) As kids, our favourite accommodation was defined by proximity to the sand. No roads to cross and we felt like we'd won the lottery, walking to the beach without Mum and Dad. We could name all the buildings along the beachfront. My favourites had regal names like *Surfers Royale* and *Imperial Surf.* At around 40 floors, the really tall ones seemed impossibly high. Looking up made us dizzy and Mum said she couldn't possibly stay in a building like that.

"What's the point of paying all that money for a balcony if you're too scared to go outside?"

Mostly I remember hanging out with Dad. His broad feet and tanned legs stretching out from drawstring shorts; suits and leather shoes banished to the back of the wardrobe where—when it was time to go back to work—he would claim that somebody had gone in and shrunk them while he wasn't looking. The same joke made us laugh every year.

For one or two glorious afternoons during our stay, he would take us up to *Grundy's* above Cavill Mall. Once there, we would flush all our pocket money down the hungry slots of *Space Invaders* and *Pac Man*; and do battle in the rifle range, ears ringing and heart thumping with the thrill of it all. Once we'd emptied our pockets, we'd turn to Dad.

"Dad, c'nive a twenny?"

Shifting from one foot to the other, shouting over the noise, we'd badger Dad for more twenty cent pieces until his pockets were empty and he'd call it a day. Resting underneath the tangle of water slides at the top of the Mall, we'd lick the drips from our Flake cones and listen with rapt attention as the older kids told stories of razor blades wedged in the cracks of the slides. Someone always knew someone who knew someone who got cut.

"Honest! Dead set! You can ask them yourself if you don't believe me."

I didn't fancy finding out.

For three, sun-soaked weeks, we'd trail sand and wet towels between our unit and the beach. The surf seemed calmer to me in those days. Perfect breaks that would sing out to be ridden by body or board.

"Take me out Daaaaaad," I would whine, as soon as our towels hit the sand. "Take me ouuuuuuut."

First, he would attend to the umbrella, setting up camp for my mum and sister to work on their tans. Like the perfect roast, this involved hours of careful basting and turning at the correct intervals to achieve a deep, golden shade. The sweet smell of coconut Reef Oil sizzling in the midday sun. The first peel broke the seal and after that you could get yourself really brown.

Not that I spent much time sunbathing. After setting up the umbrella, it would be my turn. I would follow Dad down the sand, walking one pace behind him so I could fill his footsteps with mine, believing that if I did, some of his magic would rub off on me.

Once in the water, I would stick close, trying to match him dive for dive. He taught me to dive deeply and dig my fingers into the sand while the breaking waves rolled over my body. With my brothers in tow, we would swim out past the breakers, long past where I could stand. At first, I just watched. But soon enough I was catching my own waves.

Push off, kick like mad, pump your arms, stick your chest out and you're away!

Taking off on a wave was the best feeling in the world. Of course, there were many times I misjudged the conditions and would be tossed around like a ragdoll, salt water burning the back of my nose and throat. But I always came back for more. Together we would bob around for hours, like wrinkled, salty prunes; the shadows of the high-rise towers marking out the hours on the sand.

I've always loved the feeling of that first dive into the ocean. Not diving under generally or into a swimming pool. Not the second or third dive. Singularly the first, when you enter that salty cocoon, the temperature is at its most shocking and your mind is stilled with the effort of just trying to make it back up to the other side. Eyes closed, the thin veil of eyelid no match for the force of the Queensland sun.

The orange hue behind your eyes heightening the sensation of being touched all over and at once by the water's frigid embrace. Muted sounds rush past your ears, the low rumble of the wave mixes with your own exhale. Then suddenly, the spell is broken as you burst through the surface to the other side to take a deep breath and lick your salty lips.

I grew up with sand in my togs. Hair you couldn't brush out. Skin that blistered and peeled. I'd always felt like the beach was part of me. But we had to endure some time apart, the sea and I. At 24, I packed my bags and headed north. Far north into the hemisphere above, where the sun shone for eighteen hours a day in summer but the water was freezing all year round. In the eight years I lived in Scotland, I didn't ever dip so much as a toe in the North Sea. On my return to Australia each year, I would flee to the beach and savour that first dive into the ocean.

Hello my old friend, I'm back again.

Over the years, I've tried to introduce my husband to how I spent my childhood. Long days at the beach, salt crusted skin. I've longed for him to love it as much as me. To understand the freedom of the ocean. To know the exhilaration of riding a wave with nothing but your chest, hands and feet. But growing up in the hills of Scotland, he never got the chance to love it like I did, before the ocean took that dream away.

It was holiday time again and this year, we had taken our family reunion further north. Away from the crowded Gold Coast beaches, *Ripley's Believe It or Not!* and souvenir shops. Away from the buses disgorging tourists for their designated photo stop, squealing with a mixture of fear and delight as the waves licked at their rolled up jeans.

Away too from the safety of the red and yellow army, their vigilant eyes in watchtowers all along the familiar stretch of beach.

Just south of Mudjimba, on the Sunshine Coast—a sleepy hamlet on the northern edge of the Maroochy River, where kids still play cricket in the street—it was like time stood still. Apart from a few dog walkers in the morning and fisherman at dusk, even on the most perfect days, the beach at our end, near the mouth of the river, was deserted. The five minute walk through the airless paperbark trees to reach the dunes put most people off, preferring instead to splash around in chlorinated pools at the holiday resort.

"Take me out, Dad?"

It's one of two questions that could strip away the years. The other would have him digging in his pocket for his wallet. "Inflation!" he'd cry, with a wry smile, as he handed over a twenty dollar note.

I knew Dad was an easy target for a 'real swim' because he loved the ocean like I did. (Or rather I loved it like he did, because he taught me how.)

I cajoled my reluctant husband too with the lure of teaching him to bodysurf again. A few years before we'd spent a magical afternoon catching waves at Wategoes Beach, Bryon Bay. The conditions were just right, the gently curling waves fooling us that body surfing was easy and we were any good. For the first time he'd seen what I see and felt what I feel.

"I reckon I'm probably Scotland's best body surfer!" he'd boasted.

"Probably Scotland's only body surfer!"

He still whinged about the sand and sun cream, but in the end, he relented.

The three of us surveyed the beach and dropped our towels on the sand. There were a few people walking in the distance, but as usual, the beach was ours.

I pondered the nearest flags. I thought there may be some up at Mudjimba but that was at least a twenty minute walk along the beach. Twenty minutes too far in my heat-addled state. I just wanted to cool down. The urge to get my head underwater was like a magnet pulling me in. But before I could experience the sensations I craved, I had to get in first.

If you've ever watched people entering the water at the beach, you'll have likely seen three types of swimmers emerge. Usually young guys, 'splashers' like to make an entrance by cavorting around, spraying freezing water all over their friends or unsuspecting girlfriends, before belly flopping sensationally onto the nearest wave.

Calm and focused, 'professionals' enter the water with purpose, giving nothing away about the water temperature and seemingly without noticing the people around them. Usually fit, they look like they do this all the time. Probably because they do.

By far the most entertaining, 'dancers' aren't trying to be funny at all. From the moment the first toe dips in the water, we can read their thoughts in every movement. Entering the water on tippy toes.

Eeeeek! It's freezing!

Stomachs pulled in, contracting their bodies away from the cold, splashing water.

I'm not sure I can do this!

Getting into the water can take up to ten minutes, gaining centimetres at a time, until finally, they muster enough courage to dive in.

I'm going in, even if it kills me!

Or they give up and abandon the swim completely.

I didn't really want a swim anyway.

Then, and now, Gold Coast beaches are punctuated by yellow towers, home to hundreds of sun-bleached professional and volunteer lifeguards who donate their weekends to the rest of us. Eyes in the tower. In the truck. On the sand. Every 500 metres, the red and yellow flags mark out pockets of safety, like a security blanket thrown over the waves, where you can swim with a back-up plan.

Here, there was no-one telling us where to swim. Not a single structure was visible on the scrub-lined beach. No development, no sign of humanity anywhere. But I didn't worry too much. I was with my dad. And so we walked past the stretch where the lifesavers would have planted the flags. Past the spot where the beach safety information board would have read: Unstable conditions close to shore. Deep water in close. Flash rips sweeping north. Stay on your feet.

Dad sauntered down to the water's edge. His tanned body and signature black Speedos unchanged with the passing of years. I was transported back to the beaches of my youth. Like a true professional, within seconds he was in and under, making his way out past the white water. We followed after him. (But first, there was the matter of a little dance...)

I sucked in a deep breath and dived under. Thoughts slipped away. Time slowed. Lightness took over my mind and body. I felt free of tiredness that fogged my new-mother brain. Free of expectations. I dived again, trying to recapture the feeling but it was already gone, slipped away out of reach, waiting for me next time.

We headed out to the sandbank and sought out waves with varying success. We kicked off the bottom and swam hard but the waves weren't powerful enough to get us going.

The tide was retreating, and so were our towels, getting further away as we drifted up the beach in a strong northerly sweep.

Dad pulled the pin first, catching his last wave.

"Had enough?"

My husband nodded and we started to go in.

Had we been standing on the beach, we would've seen the dark blue track running between us and the shore. A painter could spend days mixing colours to recreate the different trails of blue. But I saw nothing and made my way off the sandbank first, not registering the deep gully that had formed. The bottom fell away quickly and I could no longer stand. I turned to see my husband follow my flawed path.

"Hey, what happened there? I can't stand up!" he shouted, treading water a few metres from me.

"We're in a gutter," I called. "Just keep swimming in!"

I tried freestyle but got nowhere, the sweep making my effort null and void. I swam sidestroke with my eyes trained on the scrubby dunes, measuring our progress against the line of trees. Even without the familiar high-rise landmarks, I could tell we were making no headway at all as the swell swept through the deep gutter and dragged us sideways out to sea.

We'd already been in the water for almost an hour. My arms ached. I could see that my husband was trying hard but his eyes were growing wider as each wave passed through, slapping teasingly against his head and shoulders, pushing us further away from our goal.

Dad was on the beach, walking towards our towels. His back to us.

Turn around! I willed him. *Turn around!*

He hadn't yet noticed my cardboard box floating out to sea.

"Daaaad! Help!" I stuck my hand straight up in the air, appealing to the surf lifesavers who weren't there.

And I swam, kicking furiously with each passing swell. Finally, my foot caught the shelf on the other side. My toes curled, clinging desperately onto the sand. I dragged myself up the bank and suddenly, surprisingly, I was in water ankle-deep, just metres away from where husband was still stuck in a watery hell.

"C'mon!" I shouted. "You're nearly there! Just a few more kicks!"

I'm not the strongest swimmer. As a child, learning to swim was a pretty grim affair—hours spent doing chlorinated burps and chasing my own vomit around a suburban pool—but I was acutely aware I had years of experience over him.

He was treading water, completely spent. Moving just enough to keep his head above the waves. He dipped under, broke the surface and drifted further away.

I'm going to lose him if I don't do something quickly.

Without thinking, I sunk back into the water. I didn't dare take my eyes off him. I quickly reached him and looked back at the shore.

Oh God, what have I done? This could take both of us.

I saw our daughter's face and pushed the thought aside.

Stay calm.

We stayed there, treading water side by side.

"It's fine," I said to him. "We're going to get out."

"It's pretty fucking far from fine! We're about to drown!"

I scanned the beach, desperately searching for Dad. He was making his way slowly down the beach. I willed him to hurry up.

Can't you see we're in trouble here?

But instead of walking towards us, he approached a guy who's appeared with a surfboard, pointing over to us. Relief swept over me as I watched our knight in shining armour paddle in.

"Look someone's coming! Just hang on! Keep your head up!"

But I couldn't see him anymore. My voice was drowned out by the wave breaking between us. I thought, for a moment, that he was gone.

Even now, I'm ashamed about what happened that day. I should've known better. All those years 'out the back'. Everything I'd learned. Not worth a thing. "Didn't you swim with the rip?" asked my brother when we recounted the tale.

"No!" I replied, incredulous, still not believing my own stupidity. "We were so close to the beach! I thought if we just swam a bit harder, we'd make it."

I glanced over at my husband. For once, he didn't have a joke to match. He was quietly watching our daughter stack animal blocks; her chubby hands working carefully to pile them up, before laughing hysterically as she knocked them down, scattering monkeys and hippos all over the rug. He didn't need to speak. I knew what he was thinking. We put ourselves in danger and I led the charge. Foolish, unthinking, we risked everything. Because it wasn't much use in putting your arm in the air if nobody's there to save you.

But there was one person.

"Thank God Dad was there," I said, finishing the story. "He got a guy with a board to come and tow us in. It was bloody scary."

"You're all right now," said Dad, walking over to check the score in the Test, never one to dwell on what might've been. "Now, who'd like a little beer?"

Lately, we've returned to the Gold Coast beaches, with their reassuring crowds. Mum and Dad have bought their own holiday unit, trading Northcliffe for Main Beach, with its flash cars and cafe latte crowd. Like the entire coast, the beach between Southport to the Spit has taken a beating in recent years. But it's still a beautiful stretch of ocean, perfect for the grandchildren, who are busy making their own memories of summer days spent on the sand, falling in step behind their grandfather as he lopes down the beach in his black Speedos, off to catch a wave.

The beach is a few minutes' walk from the unit. Where John Kemp Street meets Main Beach Parade, you have a choice. Walk straight across onto a tantalising stretch of empty beach, or walk a few hundred metres up to *Southport Surf Club* and join the hordes of swimmers jostling for position between the flags. Teenage boys trying to impress girls, nervous parents watching toddlers, kids trying out their first boogie boards.

Each time we visit, I walk onto the beach and greet her empty beauty. I think back to the time, before *that* day, when I wasn't scared of the ocean—of what it could take away. Back then, I would've run right into the water, without a care in the world. But I'm just not that girl anymore.

And so I call the kids away from the water's edge; and we head up the beach, towards the flags.

SNAPPER ROCKS

Elli Housden

"**B**ut you promised." Felix pouts at his sister. "I want an ice cream now."

"Later," Angie says firmly. "Let's go to the beach."

"Beach," says Felix. That magic word.

At the sight of the ocean he breaks into song. "Oh, I've sailed the seven seas."

Wisps of hair blow over his forehead, eclipsing his pale blue eyes.

"Let's look for Moby Dick," Angie says, taking his smaller hand in hers. "Remember that song?"

"Jonah he lived in a whale," Felix sings boisterously. He remembers songs and hymns. And he loves to sing. They learned the song at Sunday School. A place their mother sends them every week, even though she's never been a churchgoer herself. "Do as I say, not as I do," is her maxim. Now, Felix knows the words to all the songs and hymns.

"My happy boy" is what their mother calls Felix. He has fine blond curls and wide eyes, like a pair of aquamarines. Angie longs to be called something special too. Why doesn't her mother ever call her 'my little angel' anymore? She used to be her mother's angel and her father's doll.

Totally uninhibited, Felix reaches the crescendo of his song. "Wha-a-ale," he finishes and looks to his sister for approval.

"Shh," Angie cautions, though there is no-one nearby. Except a man, who stands a few metres away, looking at the ocean. Hearing their voices, he turns, and then zips his parka over his thin frame. A bucket and a fishing rod lie at his feet.

"I'm going to catch a whale," he says, looking at Felix, a slight smile forming on his lips. "With my fishing rod. Wanna watch?"

"Yes, yes," Felix choruses, looking up into the man's unshaven face, unafraid of whales or strangers.

"Will it smell?" Angie asks, caught up in the prospect of adventure.

"Like the sea," the man reassures, "or a fish."

Angie looks the man up and down. She knows she should turn around and march her brother straight back home, before her mother discovers their absence. Yet something impels her. "Yes. I want to see a whale. Or a big fish." Anyway, she tells herself, we're just going down to the water's edge. It can't hurt. We won't drown.

Before she knows it she is carrying the rod, while Felix is holding the man's hand and running along beside him. Angie watches as the red bucket in the man's other hand swings around as he walks, and the knife inside it clatters noisily. We'll only stay for a little while, she tells herself as the man leads them towards the water's edge.

When they emerge from the gloom of the coastal vegetation, the sun looks brighter than ever. The tide's coming in and the breeze is beginning to whip up white caps, even on the shoreline.

"C'mon." Angie grabs Felix's hand and half drags him towards the water's edge. By now he's whooping joyfully. The sound carries on the wind and the man looks around to see if anyone is watching. But the beach is deserted, except for two people walking a dog, too far away to hear the children's shrieks of delight. The man picks up the discarded rod and the bucket that holds the knife he uses to clean and gut his catch. It's so long since he's been in the company of exuberant children that he's a bit nonplussed by their enthusiasm. They must be locals who live close by in the Coolangatta area. You'd think they'd be used to the sight of the sea since they live on its doorstep.

Already, both children are soaked to the skin, just from dancing around in the shallows. Angie is twisting about, burying her feet in the sand, when she feels something hard against her toes. Reaching down, she brings up a Pipi shell. She hands it to the man. 'These are good for bait, my dad says."

The man nods and drops it into the bucket. By now, Angie has decided to regard this quiet man as a friend. He hasn't spoken since they left the car park, but she's watched him as she walked behind him. Although she doesn't know the term 'body language', she feels safe in his company.

And Angie knows that it's too late to worry about her mother. Their absence has probably been discovered by now. Knowing her mother's daily routine, Angie waited till after lunch to escape with Felix. Poor little Felix, who loves to swim and build sand castles. After lunch, her mother always goes into her bedroom for a nap. Ever since their dad left, a few weeks ago, Mummy has been very tired, sleeping late and staying in her nightgown all day. Lucky it's the school holidays or Angie would fret about being late to school.

"I'm going up north, Doll," her dad told Angie, the day after Christmas. "For a while. You can come and visit me soon." That seems like years ago already, and aside from a single postcard of some coral and tropical fish, Angie has not heard from her father.

With any luck her mother has fallen asleep and they'll be back before she wakes. That happens most days after she has a few glasses of sherry with her lunch.

Anyway, it's now too late to worry. May as well make the most of the freedom, Angie decides, looking at Felix, watching him enjoying the experience of being away from home. The long summer holidays are dragging for her, with her mother too sad to take them to the beach or to one of the theme parks further north up the coast.

Felix is standing beside the man who is ankle deep in water. Angie watches him as he casts out with his rod. "Where's the whale? I want to see the whale," Felix says, pulling on the bottom of the man's tattered shorts.

"Oh, he's out there," the man says, pointing towards the horizon. "Why don't you call out to him? What's his name?"

"Moby Dick, of course," says Felix, wondering how anyone would not know that.

"Of course," the man says, remembering. "He's a giant."

By now, Angie is bored with whales and fishing. They were just a lure, to entice Felix onto the beach, to distract him from the ice cream she's promised him.

"Let's go for a walk to the rocks," she suggests.

Felix is torn between the thought of whales and the memory of the little creatures that lurk under the surface on the rocks. Finally, a certainty wins against a doubt and he latches his hand into Angie's and they disappear in the afternoon haze.

With the breeze buffeting them, Angie and Felix weave their way along the shore and between the rocks until they come to the rocky headland that juts out into the sea. Some of the outlying rocks are already covered by the incoming tide, but the sun is still shining in the late afternoon, making the little trapped pools between the rocks look as enticing as ever.

Angie and Felix poke around, dipping their feet into the deliciously warm water, taking care not to slip on the mossy green seaweed that is floating across the surface of the rocks. They are in a world apart, where parents, even fishermen don't exist. The fading sunlight doesn't bother them. Angie doesn't notice the tide changing, the rocks slipping beneath the water, the water creeping up behind them.

She is showing Felix a baby sand crab in a larger deeper pool. One tentacle is protruding from under a slimy rock. They're bent over trying to shift the rock when it happens. Their heads are level with the water in the rock pool when a large wave rushes past, washing over them and then dragging, dragging. Angie grabs onto the rock with one hand and to Felix with the other. Both feel slippery.

"Fe-e-e-e-lix." Her voice dissolves into the wind and the wave. She grips the rock to steady herself, and she loses her hold on him. Still attached to the rock, Angie watches as Felix is swept along like a body surfer in reverse, away from her grasp. Her hands cling to the rock as tightly as her eyes are fixed on Felix's face, his startled look, his mouth opening in a scream that is drowned in the wind. Angie knows that she has lost him, but she cannot look away. She has never seen him frown before, except in concentration, but now he is frowning at her, two round eyes receding, and then disappearing with the rest of him, into the swell.

This moment will be imprinted on Angie's conscience forever, and though she's just twelve years old, she knows immediately that life will not be the same again. Yet she lies there, unable to move, unaware of gentler waves lapping over her, her mind racing around the reality, the unreality of the situation. If she lies there long enough, maybe Felix will be returned to her. She is prepared to wait. She cannot imagine life without Felix. If she waits long enough, the sea might beach him like a baby whale.

What is her role in life if not to nurture her little brother, to make up for the inadequacies of their mother and their absent father? Felix is too young to understand the change in their mother, as a result of their father's desertion.

It's getting dark now. Angie lies, looking out at the ocean. She is soaked, her body soft and spongy. Reluctantly she moves, getting up before the tide takes her and joins her with Felix. Now, the sand is cool under her feet, though the wind has died. Something tells her not to walk back in the direction of the fisherman. She doesn't want to be asked questions. She's not ready to face the truth. Not yet. She needs time.

Angie moves up the beach. She walked here often, with her father when she was small. How she wishes she'd escaped on her own today. But she wanted to give Felix a treat. She feels in her pocket for the gold coin she took from her mother's purse. It's still there, tucked in a corner. Angie has no compunction about taking her mother's money. But she wishes that she'd bought Felix the ice cream cone he'd dreamed about. Before....

Angie is not afraid of the dark, nor of anything that might be hiding in the sand hills. The tree snakes that sometimes dangle from the native foliage like slender vines are buried now, under leaves or within fallen logs. Any scuttling noises will be possums or bandicoots. What Angie is afraid of, is the thought of going home. How can she return without Felix? It's all her fault. She beguiled Felix with promises of ice cream, with stories about whales and the magic of the sea. Now the sea has swallowed her baby brother up, like Jonah in the song. How can she explain this to her mother? The words that are in her head can never be spoken out loud.

Angie has no choice. She makes her way to the parking lot. The man will be there. She saw his van earlier. And it is still there, parked in a corner of the lot. As she skirts the grounds she can see the man, the fisherman, bent over, squatting on the grass, cleaning a fish. Angie wants to rush over and throw herself on him, this simple man she hardly knows. And tell him her woes. If only he was her dad.

Instead, she stays hidden behind a tree, watching the man wash his hands, wipe them on his pants. Angie melts back into the shadows and retraces her steps. She tiptoes towards his battered yellow van, tests the passenger door, opens it quietly and slides in, climbing over into the back section. The back seat has been removed and there are piles of clothes and tools and bedding in there. Angie is still damp and cool. She rolls herself under a sleeping bag. The surface beneath her is hard, a well-worn carpet.

Lying there, she is tense, especially when she hears footsteps. The man opens the driver's door. Angie hears a clatter of crockery and cutlery landing on the passenger seat, and then the man slides into the driver's seat. It's only when the engine roars roughly into life that she allows herself to drift off to sleep.

I hope he's heading north. That's her only thought before she loses consciousness.

I'm going to find my father, up north, she thinks. *My father who loves me.*

Angie dozes. She wakes intermittently, conscious of bumps and the rhythm of the winding road, and then of the lights of the M1 as the man turns north onto the highway. Disturbed by these twists and turns, she feels sore as well as exhausted. Under the sleeping bag, she's warm enough, but she's also very thirsty. How long is it since she's had a drink of water? She puts the thought out of her mind and drifts off again, dreaming of water, water lapping over her, being underwater, seeing Felix's watery eyes receding from her and then disappearing from view.

When she wakes again there's a siren. She feels the van jolt, swerve and then stop. Flashlights in the windows. Loud voices. Sounds of protest.

She rouses herself and looks up. It's still dark, but not as dark as the middle of the night. The man gets out of the van.

"Driver's licence please?" she hears someone say. A policeman. She can just make out the identical dark uniform on the two figures.

"We'll just take a look in the back, mate," she hears one of them say.

"No problem," the man replies. "Bit fishy in there."

"Fishy indeed," says the policeman as he slides the side door open.

Angie slides back under the sleeping bag. Her heart's thudding like a trapped animal's. The game's up and she knows it. She wonders if the man will be angry with her. Or the police? But it's too late now.

"Who's this then?" The policeman shines his torch into her eyes and points. "The little mermaid." She blinks, blinded and then looks at the man's face. He's turned pale with shock. Then she watches as his face changes from shock into anger.

"Why you little…" he begins and reaches out to grab her arm. "I didn't know she was in there. Honestly," he tells the policemen.

The last word is spoken desperately. The man continues to stare at her like she's an apparition. "I saw her on the beach, with her brother. They watched me fish for a while and then they left. She must have…"

"Angela Meadows. Are you all right?" The policeman looks at Angie.

She nods miserably. The game is up. Now she'll never get to see her dad.

The policeman puts his hand on her arm and helps her out of the van. "Where's your brother?"

Angie bursts into tears. She knows she should tell, but the words won't come. She cannot, will never be able to use those words to describe the image in her head. She can never tell her mother that her happy boy has gone forever. She can't tell anyone, maybe not even her dad.

"It's all right," the policeman says, in a comforting tone. "You're safe now."

Then it's like one of those police dramas on television. The policeman even says the same words. Angie listens to make sure that he's got it right. "Raymond Short: I'm arresting you for the kidnapping of Angela and Felix Meadows. You do not have to say anything, but..."

Angie stops listening when she hears her name, and she winces when Felix is mentioned. She watches as handcuffs are fixed to the man--Raymond's--wrists. Now they are pulling him towards the police car, its blue light still flashing.

Raymond Short turns, looks at her. "Tell them," he pleads, "tell them the truth."

But Angie is led away. She says nothing, just holds on to the policeman's arm and follows.

There is a second police car. She is bundled into the back of it, still clutching the discoloured sleeping bag, next to a policewoman who introduces herself as Liz. As they drive off, Liz takes hold of her hand. She has a large hand and her uniform is stretched over her large frame so that her knees show beneath her skirt. She looks like a mother. She sounds like a mother when she says: "You're safe now, Angela. All we want is for you to be a good girl and tell us the truth. Then we can take you home to your mother."

A good girl? But she is not a good girl. She is a bad girl, a frightened girl. She wants her father. She would rather be lying alone in the back of Raymond Short's van than trapped in the back of a police car with Liz. She does not want to go home, ever. The thought brings tears and she sobs loudly. It's as if the tide has burst within her. She's sprung a leak. All that water, flowing now, from her. Then she begins to hiccup. All she can see is Felix's face, the seaweed, his eyes. She wants to say his name but she can't frame the word.

Liz puts her arm around her, makes comforting noises. Angie buries herself in the seat, pulling away. "There, there, you've had an awful fright. But you're safe now." Liz whispers.

They park outside a large building. The word 'Police' is illuminated in blue. She watches as the other police car parks a short distance away, and the man, her friend, is disgorged from the car roughly, and led away out of sight.

As they go inside the police station, into a brightly lit hallway, she sees her mother sitting on a chair in an empty room. "Angie, oh, my angel." Her mother rushes forward. There are tears in her eyes. "Thank goodness you're safe."

Her mother crushes her in her arms. "Where's Felix?" she asks. Angie looks at her, a look of fear, of dread. "Where is he? Where's Felix?" She begins to shake Angie until the policewoman, Liz, intervenes.

"She's in shock, Mrs Meadows," Angie hears Liz say. "We have to treat her gently. Take it slowly. She may not remember everything that's happened, not for a while. We have a counsellor..."

Angie opens her mouth. "Felix," she says, tears running down her cheeks. She looks around. She's so thirsty. "Water," she says. "Can I have a drink of water?"

The policewoman fetches her plastic cup full of filtered water from the water cooler in the hallway. She drinks it in a single gulp, conscious of her mother looking at her.

"We were going to find our father," she says, to Liz. "He was taking me to my dad."

Both Angie and Liz watch her mother's reaction. It's like she's been punched in the stomach. Winded.

"Is that what he told you?" Her mother is horrified. Angie watches Liz's intake of breath. Then she watches as Liz writes down her words on a notepad that she holds on her lap. She watches her mother too, seeing her grief and guilt.

"That devil," she hears Liz say under her breath to her mother. "Don't worry, Mrs Meadows. He's in custody now."

"Angel." Her mother leans towards her. "Where is Felix? Where is my happy little boy?"

Angie looks from Liz to Mummy. The devil, she thinks, remembering the Sunday School lessons. And Jesus. She sees it now, the window of opportunity, the escape clause. She gets up and, pulling the sleeping bag behind her, crawls onto a sofa. She feels safer there beneath the sleeping bag, where her mother can't reach her. "I don't know. I can't remember," she says, closing her eyes tightly.

"Angela Jane Meadows," her mother shrieks. "Where is Felix? Did that bad man...? Oh where is my happy boy," she wails.

"Be patient, Mrs Meadows." Angie hears the policewoman speaking in a low voice. "We'll know more soon. Felix may just be lost and unharmed."

"Oh, really," her mother screams. "Why isn't your father here when I need him?" She collapses into the nearest chair.

Angie hears her mother, still crying. The policewoman continues to comfort her. As she drifts off to sleep, the last image Angie sees in her mind is a pair of eyes. Not Felix's eyes. No. They have been replaced by other eyes, tortured watery eyes. The eyes of the man she now knows as Raymond Short.

PULPED FICTION

Janis Hanley

"It was the best of times, it was the worst of times.
It was the age of wisdom, it was the age of foolishness...."
Charles Dickens, A Tale of Two Cities, 1857

It was the time for closing. Charles shut the door behind the last customer leaving the cafe of his book museum. He'd just started cleaning up when the doorbells jangled. "Damn, forgot to lock it."

"Hope I'm not too late?" a deep voice drawled.

Charles looked up and grinned. "I'd know that Yankee twang anywhere. How ya doin', Hank?"

"Bit jet lagged, but, hey, never been better!" Hank grasped Charles's hand between his own two and shook it vigorously.

"Come sit down." Charles pulled out a chair.

"Na, thanks. Just dropping off some old magazines I found in the factory." He took the shopping bag off his shoulder and put it on the table in front of Charles. "Present for you!"

Charles grinned. "Thank-you, Hank. Too kind." He peeked in the bag. "Very nice!"

"Better in your book museum than pulped in Detroit. Anyways, gotta go. Susan's waiting for me to take her to some fancy diner," he patted Charles on the shoulder. "All good for the big show?"

"All good. Trust me, Hank. I'll be there."

"I trust you." Hank patted Charles on the shoulder as he left. "See you then, son."

Charles stood in the doorway and watched Hank disappear into the Coolangatta crowd. It was day three of Coolie Rocks, the annual ode to cars and fifties nostalgia. Nighttime was extra crowded, the street a smoky haze of hot rods, leather jackets and polka-dot skirts. Many wore Model T Ford Centenary t-shirts. They stood out from a distance with the '2025' lit by colour-changing diodes. Some had flashing earrings to match.

Charles got on with wiping down the museum's cafe tables. It was midnight when he slumped into his chair to deal with his mail. Most were from other Book Bankers, collectors of the printed word. The daily stats on books destroyed since books stopped being printed were climbing steadily. Charles skipped over usual blogs about libraries and archives dumping their collections, cashing in on the soaring price of pulped paper. He just couldn't come to terms with government institutions seeing these collections as a cash cow to be milked. Charles always cringed at the mantra 'digital will do'.

A message from an ArthurCClarke01 attracted his attention. Most Book Bankers used a handle of a famous author, but the subject line drew him in, "Worst fears". He opened the message 'Conclusive evidence of what we've all been fearing', was all it said. Charles clicked on the link. It navigated to the Amazon book store, opening to the first page of his favourite book, Dickens, *A Tale of Two Cities*.

Charles read and reread the words on his tablet. 'It was the best of times, it was the age of wisdom…'. A whole phrase was missing. "What happened to the 'worst of times'?" he said aloud. How could Amazon books change the opening of a classic? He navigated to the Amazon Store directly and opened the book. It was the same. He went to another edition—same again. He checked every version, his anxiety building with each one. By the time he'd visited every store online, and seen every book altered, Charles was still in a state of disbelief, but he realised it was for real. The tightening in his gut suggested the worst of times were yet to come. He must show Marcel.

Charles locked up, set the museum security, and stepped onto the street. His nostrils filled with petrol fumes as someone revved an iridescent purple Mustang outside. Even Charles, who wasn't exactly a car person, revelled in the sounds and smells of real cars, now mostly absent from the streets. He took off down the street, stepping around a drunken Elvis spewing in the gutter. Elvis barely missed a beat as his entourage of doll-faced girls dragged him on.

Charles swiped his security pass and went in the side door of Marcel's Twin Towns Pulping factory, a ten-minute walk from the museum. The factory was the perfect front for a book bank. Boxes of books being delivered, followed by bushels of pulp coming out. Marcel only pulped the extra book copies and paper waste; it disguised an ever-growing collection of increasingly rare and valuable books. This collection was huge compared with Charles's museum collection.

Charles found Marcel out back updating registers. "What's happening?" Charles asked tapping the desk.

"1,287 more books added to our 'Missing presumed pulped' list. No digital copies, just sad entries in our book mausoleum." Marcel didn't look up.

"How's the pulp market today?" Charles asked rolling a chair over, sitting backwards on it.

"Interesting. Black market's down 3 percent today, open market's steady."

"What's that mean?" Charles asked.

"It usually means insider word on large disposals by an archive."

"More shredded history?"

"Yes, more discarded ideas." Marcel looked up at Charles, "I guess that's not the reason you're visiting at this time?"

Charles told Marcel about the Arthur C. message, and got him to download *A Tale of Two Cities*.

"So, it's every copy at Amazon?" Marcel asked, opening the store on his tablet.

"Every copy I opened. Even the i-store." Charles rubbed his chin against the back of the chair as he looked on.

"Surely someone else noticed?" said Marcel.

Charles shook his head. "Not a whisper anywhere—nothing on social media channels."

"Here it is, 'Tale of Two Cities, first page.'" They both peered at the screen. Charles again felt the colour drain from his face.

"It's word perfect," Charles said, pulling out his own tablet. He checked and double-checked his mailbox. "It's gone, the message from Arthur C.'s gone." Charles looked up at Marcel. There was no look of surprise, just Marcel's usual cool demeanour.

"Well, either there's an interesting new virus, or it really is the start of what the book bankers have been fearing." Marcel said, tapping away on his keyboard.

"Why would someone send this to me?" asked Charles, returning his tablet to his satchel.

Marcel shrugged, "Because you're a Dickens freak?" Marcel tapped the screen a few more times, then leant back in his chair. "ArthurCClarke you said?"

"ArthurCClark01."

Marcel shook his head. "No book banker with that name or handle." Marcel leaned forward in his chair. "How 'bout I do some more checks?" Marcel tapped away, not waiting for an answer.

"Thanks mate. I'll get going. We're open for breakfast at seven. Catch ya." Charles headed out.

"Yep," Marcel eventually responded.

Charles rounded the McLean street corner. The sun was just peeking above the sea wall, highlighting nearby clouds orange. Tall Norfolk pines loomed as ominous black sentinels under the neoned sky. Charles was relieved to see lights were already on in the museum's cafe. After the usual good mornings, Charles moved on through to check all was ready for the day. The grandeur of the nineteen-forties building came to life in the main reading room, with its geometric Art Deco ceilings of the Jazzland dancehall. Book-stacks followed its edges, scaling the walls. No books were for sale—or even borrowing. People came to the book museum for the pure pleasure of holding a book in their hands, smelling book smells and turning the pages.

Charles entered the white glove room. He straightened up the post-war Vogue pattern books—a new acquisition. They were proving very popular with the fifties fashionistas. A pile of car manuals and Hot Rodder magazines were stacked at the check-out desk. Charles collected them up, returning them to the hanging files along the back. The fortnight of Coolie Rocks was all about the iconic, largely extinct car. His customers were very sentimental about petrol cars. The silent Solectric cars that took their place, left a soulless emptiness in the streets.

Charles switched the security to daytime, activating the doorway scanners. He checked his watch. Just enough time to dash home. As he headed out, Charles ran straight into a man in a tweed jacket. The impact knocked off the man's fedora. "Very sorry," Charles said as he bent down and picked up the hat. He gave it a quick dust and handed it back. "Bit early for breakfast, mate."

The man put his hat back on, pulling the front of the brim to secure it. There was an uncomfortable moment as he searched Charles' face before speaking, "Charlez Hutton I take it?" There was a slight Eastern European accent.

Charles returned the stare, trying to recall if he'd met this person before. The man clearly wasn't a local. "Who's asking?"

"Does the name ArthurCClarke mean anything to you?" the man asked.

Charles frowned, then quickly covered it up with a wide grin that always looked too big for his face. "Of course! 2001 Space Odyssey. How could it not?"

The man cocked his head, "You received a message last night, no?"

Charles didn't acknowledge anything. The man offered his hand, "Jules V., shall we say a friend of ArthurC?"

Charles felt clueless about what to do.

"How 'bout we take a little walk?" Jules suggested.

"Okay." Charles checked his watch. "C'mon!" Charles headed for the crowded ocean-way tracks. He could rely on the safety of wall-to-wall joggers and dog walkers at this hour.

They crossed the road, making their way between a bright yellow '37 Chevrolet Roadster, and a '54 Hudson Hornet. The cars' owners were all set with chairs and umbrella, munching onion laden sausages wrapped in bread. Charles and Jules headed past the surf club, picking up the Greenmount path.

Jules cleared his throat. "Arthur works for Amazon Internet. You received an intriguing email yesterday, no?"

"Amazon!? I thought I had. The message seems to have disappeared." Charles's voice was edgy.

Jules continued, "Arthur is part of a highly confidential project. Last night was a test."

"Confidential? Surely changing the opening of Dickens is like shouting from the rooftops," Charles said.

"Not if it's only for you," Jules replied.

"Why go to that trouble for me?" Charles said.

"What if I told you that it wasn't any trouble?" Jules said.

Charles stopped. "What?"

Jules turned to Charles. "Think about our devices, the apps, constantly updated. Who ever questions what might be being delivered, my friend?" Jules paused. "You know the story of the monk who asked how to cover the world in leather?"

"I do. You cover the soles of your feet in leather instead of the world."

"Exactly. So, young man, what's the one thing you can guarantee everyone uses online?" Jules asked.

"The browsers? They messed with the Internet browsers?" Charles replied.

"Soon to be browser, singular."

"WebHG? The new all singing, all dancing holographic web browser?" Charles rubbed his neck to relieve the tension. "One browser, many platforms."

"Yez, people should be careful what they wish for," Jules paused. "Just imagine the power to change any book, at any time, for one, or all. Even scanned documents aren't safe. All can be manipulated with a string of text!"

"Surely that would take many text strings." Charles said.

"A word here, a deletion there, accumulating over time." Jules's voice went quiet. "It could be diabolical. Just look at the trouble the translation of the single word 'virgin' in the Bible can cause—it can make a child human or divine."

Charles looked out to sea, searching the horizon.

"But I don't have it. I don't have WebHG. How could that change the Dickens text?"

"Ah but you do. Everyone does. Yours just got switched on early."

Jules checked his watch and looked around nervously. "Listen, I need to go. You can help us stop this. " He patted Charles on the shoulder. "Can I see you tonight—when your museum closes?" Charles nodded. "Take care, my friend. These are dangerous times."

Charles updated Marcel, as they wandered through the Rainbow Bay swap meet that evening. Most of the stuff was junk nostalgia, and replica parts. Occasionally an interesting book or mag shows up. Usually it's some old guy, tarp spread out displaying an odd collection of parts, badges, some signs—maybe his wife's old cook books too!

"It'll be like all those suspect digital photos," Charles said. "Who'll know what's real and what's digitally altered? This can literally change history."

"Well, we've been expecting something like this," said Marcel. "It's the main reason for Book Banks."

"Yeah, so much for our scans though," said Charles. "No good to us now."

"What do you think Fedora Man wants?"

Charles shook his head pursing his lips. "Guess we'll find out tonight."

Marcel added his own news. "The Seattle network said WebHG is being launched in two days. People will have a week to upgrade, then all former versions become inoperable. No apps, no mail, no nothing." Charlie watched Marcel's face as the pieces came together, "They're selling everyone into the holographics, when it's the Trojan for text mangling."

"Not selling, forcing," said Charles. "We do have standalone backups."

Marcel shook his head, "What's the use? You might be able to see it, perhaps you can print it on a Pre WiFi printer..."

Charles caught Marcel's drift, "Yeah, what can we do with it? As soon as it hits the Internet it will be...mangled."

"How does anyone stop WebHG? Most people won't question the updates," said Marcel.

"Yeah, everyone's so hanging out for the holographics" said Charles. "I still can't get past why ArthurC chose me?"

"Because you're a Dickens freak," said Marcel

"But I'm not the only Dickens freak in the world." said Charles.

They escaped to their own thoughts as they followed the track beyond the swap meet up to the old laser lighthouse. Marcel broke the silence. "Perhaps they did choose you, and used Dickens to get you attention?"

"What could I possibly do about this in two days' time?" said Charles.

"The Model T centenary," said Marcel. "You're lending it 'local character'. Aren't you hosting the 'world first' holographic demo?"

Charles stopped walking, and stared out at the lights of some ship on the horizon. "Shit, Marcel, you reckon that's it? I'm only introducing it and covering the Model T historic stuff."

"Who else will be there?" asked Marcel

"I dunno—it's meant to be big. Guess there'll be media there."

"You guess? Probably every news outlet in the world," said Marcel.

"Well, there's Hank Bearing too, the Ford big-shot from the States," said Charles.

"Who's he?" asked Marcel.

"I'm not sure, exactly. Remember, I'm not that into cars. I collect the books," replied Charles.

"He is a big fan of the book museum—makes the trip to Coolie every year. He's donated heaps of old mags. He dropped by yesterday evening."

"Isn't he tied up with Amazon Internet?" Marcel checked his tablet as he spoke. Charles looked over his shoulder as he skimmed the text. "Look here," Marcel pointed to the bottom of the screen, "Says he heads up Ford's digital division, the main investor in Amazon WebHg."

"Get away?" Charles's broad mouth gaped.

"So you know him?" Marcel asked.

"Yeah—you know, we chat." Charles shrugged. "He's an old guy. Grew up with cars that would last 100 years—not this disposable plastic crap. It was him that suggested I present."

"It's gotta be why ArthurC targeted you," said Marcel.

Charles laughed. "How did he know I'd even do anything about this?"

"Well perhaps that's why Fedora Man was sent." Marcel's voice was quiet.

"I dunno," said Charles. "Do we even know ArthurC is a whistle-blower?"

"Look at the evidence," Marcel counted off on his fingers. "A much touted web browser is being released in two days. It's a trojan for a tool which can manipulate any text, even a scan, being viewed by any reader, and a person called Charles, who has a vested interest in the printed word, is an acquaintance of the main investor, and part of the worldwide launch. Pretty compelling."

Charles shrugged.

"Hank's doing the museum, and me, a big favour. We haven't even heard from ArthurC again."

They continued walking, heads down, hands plunged deep into coat pockets. The wind blasted as they passed the small cove past Snapper Rocks. Charles was dead tired, but any sleepiness was blown away.

Marcel broke the silence. "If what Fedora Man says is right, your tablet might still display the dud version. I might even be able to re-engineer what they did. "

"What good's that?" Charles asked.

"We could show the world." said Marcel quietly, "You'll have the stage, Charles. Think about it. I reckon you could do it."

Charles half laughed, "I'm nervous enough about my part as it is. Don't go putting this on me."

They walked on past the groves of pandanus, standing on their tiptoes. Charles imagined the trees lifted their skirts and moved around when no-one was watching. Charles and Marcel arrived at the old lighthouse, set with powerful laser beams for night whale viewing. They lost themselves, transfixed by quiet majesty of two humpback whales breaching beyond the sandbar.

Charles tried to empty his mind of the day's events, but only managed for a moment before his head started replaying events.

Hank's face kept appearing. A whale lurched. Charles stared, his mind drifted with the creature, rolled in its wake and dove the depths. Marcel tapped his shoulder.

"Time to meet Fedora Man."

It was around ten o'clock when they got back to the museum. The whole street crowd was inebriated, and particularly animated with Jailhouse Rock. Charles unlocked the front door but had trouble opening it. He and Marcel managed eventually. "Who left a bag of flour there?" Charles flicked the light switch. The alarm was flashing, there had been several breaches. He checked the display, nothing appeared missing, but if it was black marketeers, they knew all the tricks.

"Everything looks in order," said Charles walking through the cafe. But when they looked in the kitchen, the scene was utter chaos. Plates, cups, supplies—all smashed and broken on the kitchen floor. Charles' mind kicked into overdrive.

"The tablet?" Marcel asked.

"Office desk—top drawer." Charles tossed him the key as Marcel moved to the office. But there was no need for any key. From where he stood, Charles could see the drawer upside down on the desk. Marcel held up the smashed tablet. "This the one?"

"That would be it," Charles flung an already broken plate at the wall. "Bastards! Utter bastards." Charles punched the air, his fist connecting with hanging pans, sending them clattering across the room.

"I somehow don't think it's black marketers." Marcel made sure there was no life in the tablet and placed it down.

Marcel had noticed it first, when they moved through the museum to check the collection. The back exit door was ajar. There in the doorway, resting upside down, was a very distinctive fedora.

With full force Charles kicked it to send it flying into the lane way, but instead he connected with the door, sending excruciating pain through his foot. He swore loudly. His first reaction was to punch a hole in the door, but Marcel caught his arm from behind. "Calm down, mate."

"Who is this bastard? What the hell's he playing at?"

"It mightn't be him," Marcel spoke as calmly as he could.

"How can it not be him? It's his damn hat."

"It's a bit obvious don't you think?" Marcel spoke quietly. "I can see at least three possibilities for a start."

"I don't want to know about damn possibilities."

"Hear me out, Charles. Don't jump to conclusions." Marcel bent down and picked up the fedora.

Charles stood silently, arms folded.

"Well, maybe someone's trying to stop Fedora Man and Arthur C. He was trailing Fedora Man, took the opportunity to 'take care of things', including Fedora Man—leaving his hat to incriminate him."

Charles shrugged.

Marcel continued. "Maybe, someone came looking for the tablet, made it look like mischief, and Fedora Man disturbed them. I don't know."

"So we know Jack Shit! It could all be a hoax, ArthurC, Fedora Man, the lot—it even sounds like a soap opera."

"Well it's a long way from your conclusion it's definitely Fedora Man." Marcel brushed off the fedora with his hand.

"I felt a lot better when it was." Charles paced. Emotions boiled.

"Maybe. Maybe you want to be let off the hook?" Marcel looked Charles in the eye.

"Well, yeah. Who wants to be responsible for humankind's entire literary works?" Charles gestured with outstretched arms.

"Seems like WebHG makers do—well, to have control of it," Marcel said.

"Anyway, there's a museum to run. I'd better clean this up." Marcel followed Charles back to the kitchen.

Charles and Marcel finally headed out the door. "Thanks mate. My customers might be eating off paper plates, but we'll be open for business." Two days in a row now, neither had slept. They were the walking dead as they saw the sun rise over a windswept, white-capped ocean. The chilled wind cut right through their jackets as they left the museum. They went their own ways at the end of McLean Street. Charles continued up to his flat in a sixties brick walk up. He felt the pain of each stair he climbed, collapsing into bed in utter tiredness and confusion.

Only a few hours later Charles was awake once more. He checked his phone as he crunched his way through his muesli, and saw a message from ArthurC. Charles nearly choked on a cashew.

'I'm now safe in a Russian transit lounge. Jules V. requested I send this to you. He is severely beaten but okay. Help us stop this. Please, ArthurC."

Charles flicked it straight on to Marcel even before he opened the attachment. He tapped the link on the message. The NIV bible opened in the Amazon store. Genesis 1:1 was on the screen before him. Charles chuckled. The change would be recognised by all.

Charles received a text straight back from Marcel, "Perfect!"

There was a brief exchange of messages with ArthurC, but it was seeing Fedora Man at the Twin Towns hospital that day that finally convinced Charles to make a stand. Jules V. could barely open his eyes, but they did get the message that he had surprised the museum bandits. Charles's tablet had been their aim. When they left the hospital the fedora was back in its rightful place.

Charles surveyed the crowd filling Marine Parade and glanced down at the display monitors. His lonely figure on the stage would be on all the tablet devices here and remotely. He hoped ArthurC was watching. To his left he could see Marcel, ready to interrupt the signal. Nervous, Charles glanced at Hank who was sitting in the front row. Hank nodded back, not seeming to suspect anything.

Charles spread his hands wide calming the audience, signalling the beginning. A wave of silent expectation passed over the crowd. Charles turned and circled his arms tracing a giant orb. A holographic figure appeared, the size of a leprechaun, resting in his hands. The crowd oohed. He bent down and placed it on the ground. As he drew his hands up, the figure grew until a life-size hologram of Ford's Director was standing right beside him. The crowd burst into applause. The displays switched between the image of Hank Bearing, waving from his front row seat, and the hologram standing beside Charles.

The Hank hologram crossed to centre stage, raising its hand to once more calm the crowd. With a conjuring motion a Model T Ford appeared on the stage,. The crowd went berserk.

The Hank hologram waited for the excitement to subside and cleared its throat. "That, ladies and gentlemen, is just the start of the wonders you'll create with WebHg."

He flicked the front Ford insignia. The car spun, vanished into a pixilated whirlpool swooping over the audience, then reappeared as a winged Ford, flying up in the sky until it disappeared. The screen flicked to the real Hank in the front row, now standing, clasping his hands above his head, waving them in victory.

Back to Charles on the stage. Anxiety flowed through his body. Right then he wished he too was a hologram, instead of a real live human being alone on stage. He tapped play. The time-honoured theme that signalled change played: *Also Sprach Zarathustra*—the real Arthur C's 2001 theme. Huge words in 3D started scrolling up the stage, Genesis 1:1. 'In the beginning was Ford...' A pause followed. Charles stepped sideways into the black safety of side curtains. Marcel's signal had now cut over the canned presentation. In the beginning was WebHg. And, God said it wasn't good for one mega corporation to control every written word on the planet. Any line in a book, any bookstore, any document anywhere, even scanned, can be manipulated. The screen flashed images of multiple bibles in multiple, bookstores opening to the mangled Genesis 1:1. The screen glitched, but he heard it pick up again. The message continued, "Don't update, turn off your updates, beware" but something shut it down. Charles despaired, "NOOOO, it looks like a bloody circus." He knew it wouldn't be enough.

Charles made a split-second decision, and moved back onto stage. It needed a real person appealing to their senses. Charles had no idea if he'd even have sound to his microphone. He cleared his throat. It echoed down the street. He looked down at Hank standing, seething, phone to his ear. They stared at each other. Neither man knew at that point if the other was good or bad, friend or foe. They looked at each other as if there were only the two of them in the world.

Charles spoke. "My friend Hank here in the front row—the real one—asked me about a month ago to do a segment about the Model T. He asked me to speak about that piece of technology that changed the world. No-one saw it at the time, back in the 1920's, but it was the start of a world that would become obsessed by technology and its wonders. To many, it was the answer to every desire. It wasn't really, but the dream persisted, literally driving us on, until we were willing to sacrifice our planet for it." Charles paused. He had them. The audience was with him. "Today is another day just like the day when the first Ford rolled off the production line. Soon we won't even need to exist to have a life. Holograms are way more spectacular than the real thing. We will become part of a huge web of illusion, but even worse, WebHG holds a truly evil piece of technology that means no word could be trusted again. As you've seen today, any book, document, digital page can be tampered with. Is this the future we want?"

Charles put his hand out, inviting Hank to come up on stage. Hank stood, stony-faced, and shook his head, then slowly tuned to face the crowd. He raised his hand to gesture to Charles. The crowd roared. To Charles, it was very good.

A shot rang out. Charles dived to the stage. Chaos erupted as the crowd dived for cover. A single moment of eternity passed as he awaited the pain of a bullet. There were no more shots. Charles lifted his head to look out. All seats were empty bar one—Hank, slumped over a toppled chair. Charles stared, wondering who the enemy was.

Charles batted the holographic ping pong ball with his phone. The ball skittered off the table edge, bouncing high. Marcel quickly stretched to return it, smashing the ball down. Charles didn't have a chance.

"Too good. I'll stop going easy on you!" Charles spun his phone between his fingers.

"I'm just warming up!" Marcel passed his hand through the

holographic net. "So Hank sent you the game? He's okay?"

"Yeah, shoulder wound. He's making a full recovery." Charles tapped the box. "You can set this up anywhere. Most games are there—even beach volley ball."

"So WebHG is just delayed?" Marcel asked.

"Well, there are a whole heap of court cases pending. There's talk of Amazon Internet being dissolved—too much control." Charles tapped his phone, and the balls and net disappeared. "Poor ArthurC is still in some embassy in Russia. You probably noticed his campaign to turn the text manipulation code into file protection systems."

"I doubt texts will be safe for too long," Marcel said.

"I dunno. Ford wants it guaranteed, too. They sent me a payment for damages—conditions as long as War and Peace. Apparently, the Ford Investigation team got overzealous protecting their interests." Charles switched off the game box. "They'd been spying on Amazon Internet and the WebHG project...so they trashed my iPad—and my kitchen."

"They shot Hank, their own leader?"

"Well apparently it was a car backfiring. Wreaked havoc with Hank's 'heart condition'. Pretty sure they were aiming for me though." Charles pointed to himself with both hands.

"They obviously have your sporting skills then," Marcel laughed and sat down putting his feet up. "You'll be very interested to know that the pulp paper priced almost doubled last night. Word is many institutions have put a hold on book disposal."

"Is that good or bad for the book banks?"

"Well, if the idea of book banks is saving books, it's gotta be good. It's the first time in a decade that the number of printed books has gone up. Their price, too!"

They spontaneously high-fived. "And God saw it was good...very good!" Charles grinned his wide-mouthed grin.

EMPTY CALORIES

S. Elliot Brandis

Ethan watched as Matt pulled his shirt over his head, revealing the liposuction scars on his young body. The sutures had only been small, a centimetre at most, but Ethan recognised the markings in an instant. He'd seen them before on models and sports stars, actors and businessmen. These days he saw them on most of his classmates, too. When Matt caught him looking he gazed back fiercely and scrambled to pull on a crumpled soccer shirt. Ethan looked away quickly, feeling his cheeks burn pink.

Twice a week the boys changed out in the open like this, standing behind the ancient music building on a gently sloping hill. The aged red-brick of the building's walls contrasted sharply against the artificial green shimmer of the genetically engineered grass. They said that in times of drought grass used to turn brown and hard, like the tops of their cricket pitches, but Ethan wasn't entirely convinced. He knew the cricket pitch grass was just made that way.

He surveyed the faces of the other boys, searching for a gap in their collective attention, and quickly began to undress. Panicking, his soccer shirt tangled on the way down, exposing his chubby white flesh for a second longer than he had hoped.

Ethan rotated through denigrating insults in his mind, not wanting to know if anybody had seen.

"Hurry up, lads!" Rang the cry of their coach. "You only have ten minutes to loosen up before we start drills."

The coach, Scott McKenzie, was still a 'lad' himself, a fresh-faced Scotsman who'd been working as an assistant in one of the school's boarding houses. He'd only been on the Gold Coast for three months, taking advantage of the gap year program that gave the school cheap resident staff and him free room and board in another country. Next year he'd be at university, or working an entry-level job, but for now he relished the authority he'd somehow been granted over large groups of schoolboys. He moved up and down the boundary line, keeping a soccer ball aloft with a well-practiced touch, well aware of the scores of eyes watching him, impressed.

"Gonna win this weekend, I'll make sure of it." Scott kicked the ball towards the goal. The rope fizzed as it spun against the back of the net.

Ethan finished lacing up his boots and ran down the hill towards the soccer fields. When he reached the bottom of the slope he leaped over the concrete drainage channel with an imagined athleticism. The clouds of embarrassment lifted as he strode out onto the field and hunted down a stray ball. In his mind he was Theo Bailey, or Orlando Ambriz, or any one of his favourite players.

The luminous white grass of the sideline pulsed brightly as he skirted down its edge, knocking the ball a few feet ahead of him at a time. Wayward balls flew around him as his teammates warmed up, taking pot-shots at the goal from beyond the 18-yard box, or sending in looping crosses for the awaiting heads of others.

His enthusiasm got the better of him and he kicked the ball out too far beyond his stride, allowing another boy to swoop in and steal it. Dion raced away with it, heading back towards the goal square. He was at least half a foot taller than Ethan, with calves that would make a speed cyclist feel small. Ethan gritted his teeth and chased him down.

By the time he caught up, Dion was winding up for a shot on goal. As his foot stretched back, Ethan clipped his heel, disrupting his balance. He'd seen Jon Sanders do it the night before in a World Cup Qualifier, somehow escaping a red card despite the impassioned cries of the Italians and preserving a crucial 1-0 victory. Dion's foot swung forward awkwardly and collided with the back of his oversized calf, causing him to topple over.

Ethan laughed in success and pilfered the loose ball, intent on slotting it into the back of the net, past the three boys attempting to protect it from the barrage of incoming balls. He sorted through his options as he edged closer—the top left corner, the bottom right? Or perhaps try and sneak it right between a pair of outstretched legs.

Before he could make up his mind, he felt a heavy blow. Pain radiated up his leg, as his shin-pad slid meekly out of position and Dion's boot struck bone with vicious force. Ethan fell forward on all fours, stunned as the pain bled through him in a wave of heat.

"You fucking little shit," shouted Dion amidst the laughs and jeers of others. "Think you're so fucking clever but you're just a fat little faggot."

The sun burned Ethan's cheeks as he glanced up from the grass, flustered. He scanned the grinning faces, willing someone to stand up for him, or at least offer a hand to help him up. Even the sympathetic eyes diverted when he gazed upon them. Ethan felt large hands wrap around the fat of his sides. They clawed into him before hoisting him painfully to his feet.

"So that's what this shit's for? Faggot handles."

The gathering crowd cackled like hyenas. Those on the edges were brought up to speed in whispers, leering over at Ethan through gaps in the throng.

Ethan turned from the stares and fled beyond the far edge of the field, on the side opposite the music building, where the terrain banked away sharply to meet the river. An old stone retaining wall held it back wearily.

He sat on the slope, out of view from the field, with his throbbing leg stretched out before him. He fought back tears, telling himself he was too old to cry, giving himself a headache in the process. Drops bristled to the surface regardless.

As the afternoon turned to evening, a chill descended. Cold breezes rippled the surface of the water and made their way up the bank. They dulled the sounds of training. A ball came from the field, rolling swiftly down the slope, and Scott emerged, racing to catch it before it reached the water. The lip of the retaining wall bounced it to a stop. When he saw Ethan he paused, threw back the ball and yelled out for them to carry on.

"There you are, you little bastard," he said, walking over to Ethan. "Ah, I mean that in the friendly way." He sat down next to him and stared out at the murky water. "You had me worried, y'know. I don't like my players disappearing."

Ethan mumbled in response, the emotion preventing his words from coming out clearly. Scott's hand on his shoulder encouraged him to talk, and he recounted what had happened. The homes across the river glittered as he spoke, many of them owned by his schoolmates' parents. Tall palm trees accompanied them. Their perpetual fronds held tight, keeping the gardens and pools forever uncluttered. A pampered poodle yapped noiselessly at the river.

"Aye, don't worry about those rich little prats," Scott said.

"They'd leave me alone if mum could pay to fix me up."

"Crap, and what'd you be then? Just like them." Scott shrugged. "We don't have half this shit back home. None of us could afford it. But it don't mean naught. Y'think letting some bastard cut you open and melt your fat'll make you a better player? Not even the hormones do. They just make 'em bulky and stupid. Probably have tiny wee cocks, too, but I'm sure they'll get to work on those soon enough. Graduation present, maybe."

Ethan stifled his laugh. He took in a deep breath and imagined the negativity draining out of him as he let it out slowly. He pictured a dark cloud flowing out from his lungs and rolling down into the tainted river water. It made his breath feel thick like treacle.

"Tell you what, Eth. Thursday training's in the morning, yeah? Come an hour early and we'll put some work in. Do this the old fashioned way, like." Scott paused and Ethan nodded. "Good lad, now come have a kick. We're playing a practice match, shirts versus skins."

Worry traced across Ethan's face.

"Aye, you can play for the shirts," Scott said.

It may have been the extra training, or perhaps the double maths class, but by the following Monday Ethan had begun to feel better about himself. Maths was the main reason he'd won a scholarship to the school, and he'd recently managed to sneak ahead of the Taiwanese twins in the race for that year's subject prize.

They studied maths from the standard Year 8 syllabus—Fourier series, imaginary numbers, matrices, and Laplace transforms—but still, many of the other boys struggled. The teacher, Mr Reynolds, was an older man whose thinning hair was supplemented by the thick bushels bursting from his ears.

The new science building was outfitted with 3D projectors, but Reynolds stoutly refused to use them, preferring to write on a scratchy chalkboard. Ethan had no idea where the chalk came from, or the board for that matter, as none of the other teachers used it. Reynolds had just finished a particularly complex problem when he turned around to address the class.

"Now Term Three is just as important as the others," he said. "I once had a student fall twelve positions because he stopped paying attention. It kept him out of medical school."

The class groaned, well versed in the story and equally aware that the details changed each time it was retold. Most of them would move into their family businesses anyway, selling luxury homes or wining and dining city councillors to get their development permits approved.

"Yes, Mr Reynolds, Sir," Dion said from the back of the room. "But we don't all have nice fat brains like Ethan."

The back row chuckled but Ethan didn't bite. He flipped through the textbook on his tablet, pretending to find the answer to some burning question.

Reynolds looked at him with an amused air. "Ah, you're right, Dion. Your undernourished brain does put you at quite a disadvantage."

The class erupted with giggles, which Dion attempted to extinguish with a threatening gaze. The sound of bells rang over the room's PA system, mimicking the school's now silenced clock tower. Ethan rose from his chair, packed his tablet away in his satchel, and walked down the aisle between desks. When he reached the final row, Dion stood up and blocked his path. He reached out and twisted Ethan's nipples with pinched fingers.

"Sorry, mate, just seeing if you were ready for milking."

A grinning accomplice grabbed Ethan's shoulders from behind and forced him down into a nearby chair. "Better stay and study, Ethel, or you'll never be able to afford to have your tits removed."

When only Ethan remained, Mr Reynolds waddled over slowly. His bulging stomach was tucked into his belt, giving his waist a peculiar appearance. "Still here, son?" He said, raising his bristly eyebrows. His voice rasped as he struggled to catch his breath.

Ethan looked up at him with glassy eyes, his mind again running through a catalogue of grim thoughts.

"Oh come on now, boy, don't give me that look. You must try to make yourself less of a target."

Ethan bowed his head.

"Do what I do. I've lost twelve kilos this year. All you have to do is eat healthy, it's really rather easy."

Reynolds patted his tummy with conviction. Ethan looked towards the bin, brimming with the packaging of pre-prepared meals. They were the type laced with pharmaceuticals, to fight hunger and burn fat, or so the advertising claimed.

"Oh, and for God's sake drink *diet* cola," he said, a broad smile revealing his rotten teeth, glittering like beads of oil.

When Ethan left class he had missed the chaos. Each day at lunch a frenzied flock of students raced across the courtyard, descending on the school's tiny tuckshop. There they jostled for spots in the queue, awaiting the unlocking of the finger smudged glass doors, as prefects barked warnings in vain. By the time Ethan arrived the shop was mostly empty, one of the volunteering mothers already counting the takings. Stray chips and sprinkles of salt lay scattered across the barren warming cabinet.

"Sorry, love, but most of the goodies are gone," she said, without looking up. The plastic cash shuffled through her fingers in a blur. "Plenty of healthy food left, though."

Ethan nodded and shuffled over to the undisturbed shelves in the corner, trying to recall the pyramid that adorned his cereal boxes each morning. He sorted through health bars and packets of processed fruit, assessing the descriptions carefully. A bright blue wrapper caught his eye. His favourite soccer player, Theo Bailey, stood crossed-armed on the label, staring him right in the eye.

Packed with essential energy, boasted the wrapper. *Full of minerals including magnesium and zinc.* Ethan wasn't sure what his body needed those for. He'd made magnesium burn bright in chemistry class. He added a packet of neon fruit crisps and a litre sports bottle of bright red 'power water' and made his way to the counter. The mother's puffy lips swelled as she smiled at him. Her skin remained strangely taut.

He ate his lunch outside the tuckshop, sitting on a brick ledge that ran along the edge of the building. It formed a metre wide alley between it and the shop wall, which the staff used to store rubbish.

Flies circled the black bags, sensing the congealed frying fat and imperishable meat scraps inside. As Ethan ate his food he felt a queasy feeling in his stomach, which radiated up into his shoulder to form a dull pain. The sugars made his head spin. He'd hoped nobody would see him here, eating with the flies, but Matt soon sauntered over, his hair slick and parted.

"Make room, will you, mate," he said.

Ethan shuffled along the ledge to let Matt sit down. He had a large sausage roll with crispy gold pastry, which he dipped into a glistening container of ranch dressing. Ethan's mouth watered in conditioned response.

"What position are you playing on the weekend?" asked Ethan.

"Oh, um," replied Matt, distracted. "You don't mind if I invite some friends over, do you?"

"Of course not, but I'm not sure where they can sit." Ethan looked back along the ledge. He was already sitting uncomfortably close to the rubbish.

When he looked back, Dion and two other boys filled his vision with their over-developed bodies and twisted grins, blocking the sun.

"Just make some room," Matt said, shoving him roughly with his shoulder.

Ethan slipped off the ledge and tumbled into the rancid rubbish bags. Warm fluid leaked through gaps and soaked into his shirt. When he tried to stand, Matt stood over him, forcing him back down into the muck. Dion sat down in the newly created vacancy and slowly ate his lunch. Bitter thoughts pulsed through Ethan as he closed his eyes and waited, trying not to notice the smell. Eventually, the bell tone chimed and the boys left.

As the days passed Ethan became a shadow. He would walk between classes with unfocused eyes, keeping his mind from registering the blurry faces that passed by. In class he kept silent. At lunch he ate little. During games he would shut down his thoughts and slip into another place, another world. In this haze of detachment, he'd forgotten to dress casually on the twice-yearly 'free dress' day. Instead, Ethan came in full school uniform—collared blue shirt, grey shorts, and knee-high grey socks.

All eyes locked on Ethan as he moved around the school, no longer a ghost. At lunch, he slunk into a rarely used bathroom, hoping for some time away from the piercing stares and unmuted laughter.

As he moved into a free cubicle, a presence closed in behind him. The door swung shut and Dion stood there with him, his crooked smile breathing warmth just inches from Ethan's face.

"Too clever to dress down with the rest of us?" he said.

Dion shoved Ethan, causing him to collapse down onto the vacant toilet. His pulse began to race, and the pressure in his head rose to boiling point.

"What a precious little faggot you are," Dion said, touching his face with an open palm.

The walls of the cubicle began to close in around Ethan. The florescent light overhead burned neon bright, saturating his vision with a sickly yellow glow. Dion stood over him like a demented apparition. Ethan dug his hand into his pocket and ran his fingers over a slim metal object. He withdrew it in a single motion and jabbed it roughly into Dion's hard stomach.

"What the fuck?" Dion said. His grin dissipated as he recognised the object—a laser cutter pocketed from their Industrial Technology class.

Ethan pushed harder, his thumb hovering above the small red button, and forced Dion up against the cubicle door. He said no words but his eyes spoke for him. The acrid warmth of urine permeated through Dion's black skinny jeans. His face drained white.

"Now fuck off. Fuck off forever," Ethan said.

He backed off and Dion scurried away.

Ethan sat on the grass outside the main office while adults paced and fretted inside. His mother, bleary-eyed from a double shift, had drifted in like a storm cloud. Her fluid-stained nurse's uniform contrasted sharply against Dion's father's black satin suit. The panelled glass muted their words, leaving Ethan to sit in silence. He ran his fingers through the luscious green grass, each blade uniformly precise. Its perfection was monotonous.

In the distance, Ethan saw the flicker of a single yellow flower: A dandelion. He stood and walked to it, wondering how the weed had managed to flower despite all the pesticide. A soft white seed head accompanied it.

He reached down and plucked it gently, raising the fuzzy orb up to the sun. Its spores illuminated like a halo. He held it up to his mouth and blew, watching the seeds float away into the world, with a smile.

IN THE END

Penner Choinski

In the end, she went to Sidney's study. "I just want the fear to be done," she said to him. "McLean told me you would know what to do."

Sidney made no comment on her reference to their older brother. Instead, he picked up his phone and spoke briefly, then took her firmly by the elbow and guided her into the glossy black limousine always parked outside.

They travelled together in the frigid air-conditioning, neither speaking. Ignoring her was Sidney's habit, but today she didn't care. Instead, she drank in glimpses of beach and ocean, appearing as a twinkling mirage between the towers.

Sidney escorted his sister into the building, one of his latest acquisitions. Maybe she would settle in and get room service. A nice cool drink. Yes. Then she could talk to McLean. She shivered.

"Please sign here, Ms Somerset."

She would ask for something to dull her anxiety, maybe something which could erase the fear completely. She smiled at the advocate who settled her into a wheelchair and began to push, leaving Sidney standing at the front desk. She gave a little wave, but he turned his back and walked away.

"Could I get a room overlooking Justin Park?" she asked the advocate, starting to feel a little excited. She could have a daily plan, visit the other floors, after all, she could still get around. The air was very cold which would play havoc with her bones in the mornings. Perhaps she would ask for a heater, then a cold drink.

"Here we are," said the advocate.

She looked around her. "I don't like this room. There are no windows. Is that my bed? It has wheels. I don't want a bed with wheels."

The advocate responded by smacking a button on the wall. A moment later another white-clad man came in, and together they lifted her onto the bed. "Are we going to my real room?" She asked.

"This is it," said one of the advocates, glancing at the other. "You just make yourself comfortable." Then she was left on her own.

She was beginning to think she had been completely forgotten when the advocate visited.

"Are you ready to finalise a date? It's your choice. Pick a lucky number, use astrology, whatever."

"I want a nicer room. Call Sidney. Mr Sidney Somerset. I'm sure you've heard of him. He can sort this out."

The advocate glanced down at his notes, and read out, "*Why Are You Here?* Mr S has just put 'surplus to needs.' Nope. I think you're in the right place."

After that she turned her face to the wall whenever the advocate visited. They wanted to finalise a date. She would not choose.

"Very well," said the advocate, and admitted that compliance was a grey area. But, he added cheerfully while binding Heather's wrists, they had hopes to tighten any last loopholes. Looking down at his work, he murmured, "For your own good." Then he pushed the bed down a long passageway, the wheels shrieking all the way.

"Put some grease in 'er, mate," yelled a passing doctor. The advocate merely chuckled as he negotiated the bed into a small room. She refused to look at him. She refused to look around her, or acknowledge that any of this was happening. Her heart beat so fast she barely heard the advocate say something about turnaround time. Apparently she merited extra attention. Just for her they sent in a specialist.

The specialist was appealing, even Heather had to admit, with jet-black hair and large, sapphire-coloured eyes. Hers was a face calculated to make a lasting impression. Though she seemed young, the specialist possessed an air of gravitas, business-like, yet ever-so-slightly sympathetic. Heather's bound wrists prevented her from making any welcoming gestures. The specialist noted Heather's clenched fists, and frowned. "Ms Somerset's body position is not optimal," she said to the advocate, who shrugged and left the room, whistling 'Down Under.'

The specialist swept her black cape behind her and sat down in the only chair, facing Heather directly. She dipped her head toward a small red glow on the ceiling.

"Ms Somerset, I wish to register my disapproval of your treatment at this moment. Do you understand?"

Play the game Heather, McLean whispered.

I don't want to play their game.

Nevertheless.

She released a shaky breath. "Yes. I understand." The specialist stretched her lips in an upward motion. "The restraints are only physical. Your mind is free. And that's so important, isn't it? Especially these days."

"Oh, is that the line you take?"

Let her talk, reasoned McLean.

The specialist flicked through pictos in the air. Finally she X'd out, tapped her stylus against a fingernail, and sighed. "I acknowledge that you have signed all the requisites, no relatives have filed objections, all levels completed. So…we just need you to do the end-discussion, and then we are, as we say, 'Good To Go'."

"Yes, as you say." She timidly swivelled her head. For the first time she examined the compact space, noting with rising horror tubes and stainless steel connected and leading to a perfect end, a needle so thin it was barely visible. She gasped. "What's happening? What are you going to do?"

The specialist pursed her lips and folded her arms tightly. Her eyes went to the red light on the ceiling. "Ms Somerset, how may I facilitate your compliance?"

"I…I don't know." Compliance. So this is what Sidney meant.

The specialist looked slightly annoyed. "Are you having second thoughts?"

"I don't know!"

"I detect your hesitation Ms Somerset. Maybe second thoughts, due to…?"

Go on. Tell her. Heather could feel McLean push against her mind. *We're running out of time.*

She opened her mouth, and watched the specialist lean forward expectantly.

Do I really want to start this?

Yes, yes, yes, her older brother answered impatiently. *Tell her.*

"Ghosts."

"What? Ghosts? Did you say ghosts?" The specialist swivelled to look around her, then abruptly bent forward, scooting the high-back office chair closer to where Heather was half-reclined.

Heather nodded.

"What do you mean? Ms Somerset? Could we press on please?"

"I'm trying. Trying to press on." Heather paused, studying the tiled floor.

She won't listen, McLean. She has more important things to do. The line-ups are out the door of the clinic. I saw them on the way in here. More and more every day, Sidney said.

Bet that made him happy, muttered McLean.

The specialist cleared her throat.

"I must register my warning to you at this moment, that continued non-compliance will cause ejection from this clinic and into a Life Affirming centre."

"No! No!" She had heard a rumour, nothing more, of vegetative eternity. McLean would never be able to reach her again.

Oh Hallelujah, silently crooned McLean. *Now you get it, sis.*

"I think you have made your choice, Heather. May I call you Heather?" The specialist cocked an arched eyebrow. "Perhaps you would like those straps removed?"

Heather nodded mutely. Upon release she rubbed her wrists and wiped her eyes, apologising for her appearance. "You look fine, Heather."

"What is your name, Dr....?"

"K. Dr K."

"I met a Dr K at the front desk. Are you related?"

The specialist radiated a few atoms of warmth. "Everyone always asks that. No, all the doctors in our field are K. It's an honorary title."

"Ah." Heather paused. "But what is your name?"

"My name is inconsequential and confidential."

"Then I'm afraid this interview is over."

The specialist clicked her tongue, gave a slight disapproving shake of her head, and left the room.

"I want to go home."

McLean briefly manifested and shook his head, twisting the air so that hundreds of thousands of molecules blurred in front of Heather.

That's Sidney's home. Why would you want to go back there?

The next morning, the specialist breezed in, flicking her long ponytail and neatly tucking purple stiletto heels behind the leg of her chair. She seemed to be in a good mood, humming 'Down under.' She laughed. "Can't get that song out of my head." She stole a glance up at the red eye, and her smile faded. "So, Heather. Are we getting ready?"

Heather had never felt so stiff. The night had been long. Her mouth felt glued together.

"I haven't finished telling you my story," she croaked, and she could hear her old-lady crankiness. "I want some ice. And I want to call you by your name. I want you to be my friend. So I will need a better name than an honorary title."

"In that case, I can give you some very good news," said Dr K. "I talked with the Head last night." She gave Heather a look which said: see, you *are* special to me. "You can call me Kay. "K-a-y. If that helps you."

Heather nodded. "It does."

"Then 'Kay' it is."

"All right. Kay. Where's my ice? Can't be expected to talk with a dry tongue."

Kay gestured hurriedly toward the staring red eye. Moments later the advocate appeared and slammed a cup of shaved ice beside

Heather, then turned to leave.

"Wait," Heather said, glancing down at her hands. "My wrists are very sore from the straps yesterday –"

"Sorry, love. Just don't have the time." The advocate turned to leave.

"Where are you going?" demanded Dr K. "Aren't you going to comfort our client?"

"What's the use," replied the advocate.

Dr K leapt up and followed him out of the room.

For a few minutes Heather sat in silence, watching the ice tantalisingly just out of reach. McLean could not help, though she was sure she could spy him in the radiating vapor coming through the wall vent, which wafted down, ending in a chilly pool at her feet. She wasn't alone, of that she was certain.

Dr K briskly re-entered the room, pulling the door closed behind her without looking. "Getting rather busy here," her only comment. She moved her chair close, and eased a chip of ice into Heather's parched mouth. Oh, it felt good, a small miracle.

Now. Time's come. She cleared her throat.

"I will formally begin my end-discussion."

Kay nodded. "Good."

"But there's something I have to tell you about, first."

Dr K frowned. "Very well."

"Are you recording this?"

"Recording. Continue."

"Seven and a half years ago," Heather said, "my older brother, McLean, disappeared. Vanished right off the Earth. I tried everything, private detectives, the lot. Then, last week, he contacted me. I couldn't believe it. Had so many questions. But he sounded strange. I was over the moon to hear his voice, but it wasn't right."

"What do you mean?" asked Kay.

"He was calling from home, he said. He was worried for my safety, said he had found a way for me to get out of Sidney's sphere, forever. And then he told me he had a plan. He's here, you know. Right now."

"What, here? In this clinic?" For just a moment she appeared to frown. "Not mentioned in your file. Someone has lapsed. I must register my surprise and disapproval." Kay made an obvious show of glancing at her watch.

Heather drew in a swimmer's breath.

"Listen, Kay, in order to explain it I will have to start at the beginning. 'Once upon a time' kind of thing. Once upon a time there was a poor family. This family had always known poverty, both of money and of spirit. So long had they toiled, the scope of their world (in both form and imagination) travelled only from the red dirt of Springbrook Road to the Burleigh Esplanade, along the ocean.

"Some in the family had once lived in different towns, different countries. But time smoothed away all alliances to anything but the coastal neon, grey-green eucalypts, warm salty air, and glittering sea defining all that was the Gold Coast. My town. The only place I ever wanted to be."

Heather noticed a glaze creeping into Kay's eyes. She didn't want to be dull. She must be more interesting.

"If you wanted information, you came to the Somerset house. Mostly favors were done for us, 'cause we were considered right mongrels, though the Gold Coast was full of dodgy types. Not everyone mind you." Heather smiled. "Never mind, long time ago. The 1970's. You know what they say: if you can't remember them… actually, what do they say?"

Kay raised her eyebrows and pulled a face. "Before my time."

"Have you seen the picture in my file of that fine old house in Burleigh Heads? Early Queenslander style. Right beside the church? Well, it used to be a church. Now it's a Life Affirming Centre for those who…you know…aren't ready. Anyway, the house. That was my house, courtesy of Sidney. That house was old when I was young! Wonderful for a good Aussie holiday. Now? Merely prime real estate. Politics can be…lucrative."

Dr K interrupted. "I must register that your cynicism is a mark of a bygone era."

"I am calling it as I see it."

Kay tapped her nails on the chair.

"Your attitude conveys a certain lack of acceptance. I have to register my…" Kay stopped, searching the ceiling. She bit her lip. "I am registering my apologies. Please go on."

McLean she's getting angry!

Tell her about our house, about the church, what Sidney did. She has to be told.

"All through my childhood there were bougainvilleas growing hodgepodge, scattered about, flowering through even the hardest years. A winding path joined the road, lined with sulphur-coloured wattle blooms. Lemony-scented. I see it all so clearly right in this moment. Lead-light windows on the front door, native trees up the drive, two giant Bunya pines guarding the whole front of the house. And in the back…the ocean. Nothing but the turquoise-blue sea. McLean used to be afraid of the ocean. Ran away to the bush. But, in the end, I could never live far from the water. Don't understand how anyone could. I had another brother. *The* Sidney Somerset. But you know all about him, don't you? Started the first Assistance Clinic on the Gold Coast, etcetera. McLean said that particular business was the perfect melding of man and heart—or lack of it. My brother Sidney has a lot to answer for."

Heather was staring up at the ceiling when she noticed the red eye blink. She saw Dr K touch her ear. "Can you please explain what you meant by your last statement, Heather, in which you said, 'Sidney has a lot to answer for.'"

"He does."

"What specifically do you judge?"

"Specifically? I can't say. It's McLean who has the specifics. If I judge anyone it's myself. I was always complicit, always. I see that now."

Dr K touched her ear again and nodded slightly. "That is acceptable. Just as long as you see your own place." She gestured for Heather to continue.

I've confessed and that's all she can say? For a lifetime of turning away from love?

In her head McLean spoke ruefully. *You're on the edge anyways. Might as well jump.*

"Something about churches set Sidney off. Rocks and fire were his weapons of choice. He said he knew just how much to do, so the parishioners would never be able to repair the damage. That's how Sidney got the land cheap.

"The fact was that people were enticed to my beautiful Gold and Green, bedazzled not by life, but to have a lifestyle. McLean cried about the trees which were torn down to make way for the newcomers. Sidney was always on about peak oil and providing energy for the future. Somehow, Sidney seemed more sane than McLean. At least, I thought so."

Heather stopped. Once upon a time she had seen a forlorn koala, clinging from a branch of the single gum tree in her estate park. She came to a sudden conclusion.

"We are evil."

Dr K barked out a sharp laugh, jarring Heather.

"Evil," said the specialist. "Now there's a word you don't hear every day."

Fatigue suddenly overwhelmed Heather. She lost her place in the room and was overlooking an arid valley. She called out in alarm for McLean. An inhuman scratching sound stabbed terror into her throat, and just like that she returned to the white room where Dr K was rubbing her fingernails back and forth along her armrest. Out of the corner of her eye she caught sight of a something disappearing into the wall. It almost looked like Sidney. She looked back at Kay. Did she see him too? Heather quickly continued.

"McLean liked to share his thoughts with me. He said that ultimately the individual falls before the harvesting blades of Culture. We need to run hard, exert our souls to stay ahead. I always believed he meant I had to keep my eye on the prize. I couldn't have been more wrong. Sidney, of course, twisted it into his own version: become anti-fragile. Koalas were fragile; people should be the opposite. Sidney became obsessed with that idea. He decided that he could not just ride out disaster, but become stronger through crisis. Eat tragedy for breakfast, then go for a workout. Now his political marathon makes sense, don't you think? McLean thought that being a politician just meant helping to build a bigger monster, which still got you in the end."

Kay shook her head. "McLean sounds disruptive. Are you sure he's here in the clinic?" She looked concerned. "Security is important here."

"McLean won't cause you any problems."

"You mean he's already gone?"

Heather sighed. "Oh yes. He left."

The specialist pursed her lips and brought up Heather's chart again. After flipping through page after page, she finally stopped, looking puzzled. "His name is registered…that's weird…links are all dead. There's no recording."

"Listen…Kay…I am getting to it."

"Do so."

"All right." Heather looked out the window for inspiration. She saw…nothing.

Almost there, urged McLean. His voice sounded weak, as if stretching from far, far away. *Time is getting thin.*

I'm trying to remember! You don't know what it was like, all the years and years of hiding from Sidney. You don't understand how much energy it took to keep smiling. Smile, though my heart was breaking, for you, for my dreams. You're the one who abandoned me to hide in a shed out in Woop Woop. How would you know what my life has been like?

I came back for you, didn't I?

Heather turned to Kay. "Do you really want to hear the whole story of my life?"

The specialist shook her head. "We only need your end-discussion—why you came to the clinic. And a final summary of who you are."

"You wouldn't understand."

Kay smiled. "My understanding isn't necessary."

"But, that's the thing, Kay. I want you to understand."

The specialist raised her eyebrows. Her mouth formed a straight line. "I am here to facilitate your compliance. Once you have entered the clinic, then a certain set of events are set in motion. You have already agreed. You must comply. I'll do my job, get you good to Go."

"You're annoyed with me."

"No. But I desire to clear my client schedule."

"I like you, Kay. I want you to like me too. It's important."

"I do like you, Ms Somerset."

"But…"

"But you are clearly not ready. Perhaps you will never be ready."

Before she could rise, Heather desperately restarted her story.

"Get this. Gold Coast Radiation Remediation conference 2021. I remember Sidney was at the podium. His speech was about McLean, the pain of watching a dear brother struggle to stay alive when all reason said, 'Let him go.' How it came to him that there should be a better way. That there should be a place where all suffering people could go to get help, where structures could serve the comfort of society. 'And thus,'" Heather imitated Sidney's voice, stretching out her arms in a mock T, "the Assistance Clinics were born, and arising with them was a resurrected Gold Coast, with a new message: 'Suffering One Day, Released the Next!'

"Sidney's colleagues applauded wildly. He spoke about those who didn't want to participate in life, how they could be helped in a tangible way. Our city would become the exit point of choice. 'We can, we will, do good through making people good to GO.' He cocked his head up at the sky and yelled, "Whattayathink?" then fist-pumped.

"It was masterful. I had to admire his power."

Kay quietly watched Heather. "Sidney personally assisted McLean to Go. Is that your problem, Heather?"

Heather took a deep breath and blew out slowly. She measured out her words carefully.

"McLean didn't want to die. He was terrified to leave the Earth. The idea of it…" She searched Kay's eyes for a connection. "McLean was depressed and wouldn't get treatment. Utterly resisted our help. He said, as the Natural world disappeared so did his will to live. But he was trying to get Sidney to change. He didn't want to die, he didn't want Nature to die, he wanted our culture to wake up to what is real. In a sad, horrible way, he did change Sidney's mind. The Assistance Clinics. Clearing away the deadwood, giving the lucky ones a better run. Now *I'm* deadwood. So you see, McLean was right: the cutting blades of culture have caught up with me at last." Heather exhaled shakily. "The last thing McLean said to me, was 'only Life matters.' I've spent a lot of time thinking about that. Years."

Kay interrupted. "You said that McLean was here. You talked to him last week. I don't understand how he can be here and yet disappear years ago. And I can't see how you could describe easing the world's pressure as 'clearing the deadwood.' You are being exasperating, and I am beginning to think, on purpose."

"This is supposed to be my story Kay. Why do you want me to change it?"

"I don't want you to change the facts. I disagree with your interpretation."

"Why do you care?"

The specialist remained silent.

"Here's some facts for you, Dr K. Sidney said that McLean was 'diverting focus'. That was his crime. I stood by. That was *my* crime. Sidney thought he was shooting McLean and all his inconvenience out into some sort of vast blackness. McLean was simply dispensed. No end discussion, and so no proof of McLean's existence."

The specialist looked stunned. "That's why there are no tags on his meta-file."

Heather nodded and began to cry. Her tears ran into her wrinkles, and the air-conditioning chilled the ridges of her skin. "Yes, McLean, you are right, it was murder. Now I see Sidney will be lost to the void."

Thank you, sis. Thank you.

"Can you see that Kay?" She exclaimed. "Can you see him? McLean wants me to come with him back Home."

"Of course he does," soothed Kay, patting Heather's hand. "We can always trust in the memories of our loved ones, right up to the end…"

"Dear McLean and his gentle soul, so much kinder than my pragmatic head. His heart connects me to his Home. The only connection I have, now. Home is, and apparently always has been, invitation-only."

Heather was almost jumping with excitement. "You could come too, Kay! Open your heart. Now McLean lives in your mind, too."

Kay pulled back. "What do you mean? I am...No, not confused. Perplexed. No matter. No, all right. No. You can say what you want, as long you adhere to our guidelines and make your exit in a dignified manner and don't eat up resources." Kay nodded emphatically and spoke directly to the ceiling.

Heather watched her sadly.

If only we hadn't wasted so much precious time to establish the truth. If only. Wasn't that always the way?

"Love is the fifth element, quintessence, the medium of life. Love is the channel to Heaven. And it must be passed on." Heather concentrated all the force of her being through her eyes and focused on the other woman's face. "Do you ever feel loved, Kay?"

The specialist stood up abruptly, and turned away. Then she addressed the ceiling. "I am registering my professional opinion that you are ready to Go. Do you accept this opinion?"

McLean stroked Heather's hair. *Yes, you do.*

Heather considered her choice: shake off McLean's hand and rejoin Sidney at his ever-so-respectable side. It wasn't too late to grovel, appeal to his ego and tell him she was wrong to doubt his vision of the Universe. Or should she simply fall into the currents of space, pulled by McLean back to his new Home? She could feel the pressure of McLean's soul against her mind, asking her to trust him. She began to remember his crazy theories and earnest ideas. She wondered if he could cloak her, making her safely invisible, forever. She began to believe that maybe her life wasn't over, just going in a new direction, and then she began to believe in him.

Heather closed her eyes and saw a perfect, shimmering wave approach the shore.

"Yes."

"Very well Ms Somerset. Let us proceed. Your summary, please."

RECORD OF END-DISCUSSION, ACTIVE RELEASE

Kay, please, hold my hand. No, don't let me see the needle. Let me see your face. Let me explain my old fear. My powerlessness has been pure torment. Dread and doom in every event, my culture was…is…an insatiable beast. My defense? Peace at *any* cost. In the end I had only god to pray toward. Was I misled? No more options. All red-dirt roads had led to the fatal canyon of dead ends. And then, against the odds, McLean came through, crystal-clear.

I ask you: where else is there to go but up? Up to the green heavens, above the never-ending cloud, that rapid transport to all those other places I have never been. Never believed I would ever go. You have to keep hope, Kay. That's the key to going home.

This age of realism…(indistinct) clear how many dreams dry from lack of nourishment, the food of our hope…am tired…justification is a road too well travelled. You have waited to hear me out and I can see the light dying in your eyes, too, Kay. But tomorrow you will wake with that pure juice, the wondrously diligent, productive you—savaging all disillusion, delusion, foresight, hindsight—destroying all forms of truth which we are capable of conjuring up in any given night. [laugh] Listen to me go on! Glorious youth-drug of nature, my girl, don't deny it of yourself. All too soon the spark can be gone and then the dreams are not worth the effort. Your brand will tarnish. The nights will feel longer. And the truths that come out of them make it harder to…remember love. [breath slowing]…my duty as an old woman to pass on that little bit, just as old women have done everywhere and every-when. [pause] Remember my recording,

Kay [indistinct]…see me again? Yes. [emphasized] Yes…home again. McLean says it's a better place. [exclamation] My house on the esplanade! Beach showers, open-air blues, the pink poodle…ibises…sea turtles. Woolly mammoths! [laugh] You would like it Kay. Gold and green and green and gold and…everything has its place. Magnificent order. The prime mover sees all and all of us from the sky without stars [exclamation] Kay, Kay you're squeezing my hand so tightly (FINISH)

PARADISE DROWNED

S.G. Larner

I crept away from camp, wading through the shallow water that flooded the mature rice crop, and climbed up a small hill in the middle of the paddy. At the summit I lay on my back. Wisps of cloud swirled across the stars. The sounds of people drifted on the humid breeze: talking, pots banging together, the cries of tired children, the occasional raised voice. Smoke from the woodstoves lingered in my hair. My conscience nagged me to go and help clean up, but instead I gazed at the sky and wished I could fly away.

Water sloshed. I tensed, then a familiar irregular footfall crunched uphill toward me. I sighed and sat up. Guilt prickled, that I'd made Layla follow me out here on her crippled foot.

"Nasra, you must stop this. You are not a little girl anymore." My sister's voice was sharp but carried a note of sympathy; at twenty, she was three years older and wiser than me.

I replied in Arabic. "Every night I want to throw up, waiting for the next one. What if it's you? What will I do then? We've already lost Mama."

The night darkened as clouds gathered to obscure the stars. The first drizzle of warm rain started to fall as Layla sat beside me. She gazed off to the east, to the hills where the remnants of the Gold Coast's residents clung, safe above the flooded streets of the coastal strip. New Venice, as it was known, was the refuge for undesirables and escapees.

"Be strong," she said, stubbornly speaking in English. *The more we speak English, the better we get.* She put her arm around me and squeezed. "We will take care of each other." She stood and tugged at my arm. "No point worrying about what might be. We take one day at a time."

I pouted but in the darkness she didn't see it. With a groan, I got to my feet and wiped the rain from my eyes.

"Good girl," she said. We returned to the camp filled with temporary buildings and unwanted human flotsam.

The Company man frowned, his face pale and narrow, as he inspected his clipboard. Heavy clouds bulged over us, dark and threatening like his steel-grey suit.

"There's been three deaths in the past month." He squinted at Mehmet, the man designated as overseer for his excellent English. He'd been a university professor in Iraq before trying for a life of peace in Australia, and held informal English lessons for the rest of the refugees. Mehmet's skin was shiny with sweat. He shrugged and stroked his beard.

"Yes, sir."

The Company man pressed his lips together until they formed a white line. "Harvest begins next week. Ensure nothing disrupts it." Thunder rumbled under his words and the smell of petrol from the ancient army truck made me light-headed.

Mehmet's jaw clenched. We fidgeted in the line as the doctors checked us one by one. The air was steamy but the clouds gave us respite from the sun. They treated the fungal infections, but ignored little Sharif's malformed lip, baby Jannat's sixth toe, and Hediyeh's weeping skin rash. If it wasn't life-threatening, the Company didn't care.

After we were given the all-clear we were sent into the paddies to spray for insects. This rice crop was scarlet rice, enriched with iron and Vitamin C and resistant to leaf-eating insects, but we still had to spray for stem-borers using hand-held pumps. We'd given up on asking for safety gear.

"It's better than waiting in Cairo for the bomb that kills us," Layla said in Arabic from behind me as she limped through the brown muck.

"Is it?" I chewed my lip, guilty again. She could have died instead of losing half her foot. More vigilant than I, she'd heard the whir of the mortar and thrown herself on top of me before the explosion. Trapped under her unconscious body, covered in rubble, nostrils thick with dust and blood, I'd been terrified she was dead.

"Or being locked in that detention centre. Remember that? The man who sewed his lips shut and died of starvation? Would you rather go back to that?"

"Layla, stop." I whacked the rice stems with the nozzle and groaned as the clouds opened. A steady rain fell, drowning out my words. "No, I wouldn't go back to that."

"We have some freedom, Nasra," Layla said, then switched to English. "For that, be grateful."

Rain beat a dull percussion on the roof of the Wajbah. Cutlery clinked and hundreds of voices created a low hum. I lined up with Layla to get my share of dinner, two ladlefuls of bland, Company-regulated slop served by gap-toothed old women who could no longer handle the hard work in the fields. A large Pacific Islander man jostled me, mumbled something and slunk to the end of the line. The stink of mud and sweat overwhelmed me until Layla, always sensitive to my moods, put her arm around my shoulders and hugged me.

We clutched our bowls to our chests and squeezed through the mass of tired refugees, mostly Middle Eastern, looking for room enough for both of us at a bench. We found a gap and sat down at a table occupied by a group of Pacific Islanders, who had fled the drowning of their homes as the sea level rose.

I leaned against Layla, sighed and picked up my spoon. A scream rang out over the din. I jumped, and a glob of tasteless, boiled rice stew fell onto the table.

"Not again," Layla whispered, and I climbed onto the hard seat to see over the heads between us and the commotion. The nearest people backed away, creating an empty space around a man and a crying woman. He rubbed her arm, saying something I couldn't hear. When he turned to her I caught a glimpse of the back of his head.

My stomach turned and I hopped down.

"Abdul's got the mark," I whispered in Arabic. My hands trembled and I dropped my spoon in the stew. "I can't eat any more."

Layla hugged me. "We'll be fine. I promise."

I pulled away from her. "Don't make a promise you can't keep."

Dawn light peeped into the girl's dormitory. I rolled slowly off the hard mattress, wincing at each squeak of the slats. I glanced up at the top bunk, where Layla slept. Her brow was furrowed even in sleep. The other girls stirred as I crept out of the building and into the morning.

Sunlight turned the thinning mist golden, wrapped us in a claustrophobic dome. At the edge of the fog, where visibility was poorest, two figures were heading away. I ran after them. They turned as I neared, their expressions wary.

It was Abdul and Marhub, his brother.

They'd been on the boat with us.

Abdul raised a finger to his lips. In Arabic, he said, "Shhh. You didn't see us."

I put my hands on my hips. "Where are you going?"

His smile was tinged with sadness. "Away from here. My time is done. I'll die on my terms." He turned and showed me the back of his head.

I hadn't seen the mark so close before. Clumps of hair had fallen out, and the small, twisted face on the back of his head was frozen in a permanent scream, like a terrifying sculpture.

A whimper escaped me. "Does it hurt?"

Abdul nodded. I raised my hand, compelled to touch it, but he turned and faced me.

"There are fences," I whispered, letting my arm drop.

"We can try," Marhub said fiercely.

"If we can get to New Venice, we'll try to get help." Abdul turned to Marhub. "Come," he said to his brother. As they disappeared into the mist he looked back over his shoulder and raised his finger to his lips once more.

A truck roared into camp in the afternoon, and grim-faced soldiers dragged Mehmet away, refusing to answer any questions. We huddled in the Wajbah, speaking in hushed voices, scared of what might happen with Mehmet gone. There was still plenty of light outside but we were done for the day. Dusk fell and the older women stirred themselves to heat the stoves and cook the stew. I chewed on my lip and debated telling Layla what I'd seen that morning.

"Abdul and Marhub are gone," she said, breaking the ice.

"Is that why they took Mehmet?"

"I don't know," she said, resting her chin on her hand and worrying at her headscarf. "Speak in English, Nasra."

"Will he come back?"

She sighed and looked down at the table. "I do not think so."

As dinner was served some of the tension leaked out of us. I dipped the spoon in the thick stew and stirred. When I picked the spoon up the boiled rice sucked at the metal.

"Layla? What if it is the food?"

I glanced up from my stew. Layla stared at me, her mouth slightly parted, her eyes wide. She dropped her spoon onto the table. At the clatter, people looked at us.

I waited for her to say something, but she seemed frozen. Then she lifted a hand to the back of her head and my stomach fell out of me.

"Layla, no," I whispered. She shook her head and clambered over the bench before hobbling into the darkness outside. I chased her, my breath coming in shallow gasps.

Hampered by her injury she was easy to catch. I spun her around, fear giving me strength. Her face was wild. "Let me go," she shrieked in Arabic.

I slapped her cheek. "Stop it!" I cried. "Stop it and let me see!"

Layla sobbed once and turned away, pulling her headscarf from her head. In the darkness I saw nothing but I raised my hand and traced the contours of the cursed face. A silent scream. The mark of death.

"It hurts," she said, her voice high and thin. "My head is squeezing, I'm afraid it will burst."

I pulled her close, feeling her body shudder with her terror. My mind whirled as I tried to make sense of everything. "Don't eat the Company food," I said. I thought back to other victims: the mark revealed at dinner, death at the next meal. "What if it's like an allergic reaction?"

"I'll starve," Layla said in a hollow voice. "It will be a slower and harder death."

I tugged at her arm. She turned without resistance. "Give me a day. It'll be like Ramadan. You can manage that."

Layla hugged me and I breathed in her warm scent. "A day. I'll fast for a day. I'm going to die anyway."

I kissed her cheek.

At morning muster we were shunned. They were afraid, so I didn't hate them, but my heart wept. The sun climbed into the sky as we trudged into the wet fields. My tummy rumbled: I'd refused to break my fast in solidarity with Layla.

There were mutters that she hadn't dropped dead yet.

"Nasra, what exactly is your plan?"

The rice stalks near harvest were tall, hiding us from view. As we walked away from the rest of our team I scanned the shallow water for signs of rogue plants. Sometimes we found a weed that managed to grow even in the flooded fields: the hostile conditions couldn't erase all signs of natural plant life. That was one of our jobs—to find and uproot any errant plants.

Layla saw the first one. She went to pull it up but I stopped her with a quiet word. She frowned at me, then something shifted in her expression and she examined it with curiosity.

"Is it edible?" she asked in a voice as quiet as the breeze. I shrugged and picked a spear-shaped leaf.

"Only one way to find out." I eased a tiny piece in my mouth. Bitterness seared my tongue and I spat it out. With a savage wrench I pulled the plant and tossed it, dripping, into my sack for burning later.

After several false starts we found a plant with floating, heart-shaped leaves that tasted mild and inoffensive. After an anxious nibble I offered Layla a leaf.

She took it, but stared at it lying in the palm of her hand. "What if it's just the next time I eat? I could be dead in a few minutes."

"You could just starve, if that's what you want." I ground my teeth together, trying to hide my anxiety.

Layla raised an eyebrow at me. Her dark eyes wide, she put the leaf in her mouth and chewed.

I didn't realise how tight my shoulders were until Layla didn't collapse and I managed to relax a little. She looked up at the sky, as if to say, *Well?*

I offered her more leaves. And then I gently lifted the plant out of the mud, roots and all, and hid it in a second sack that I'd shoved into the first. Layla smiled. "We plant it somewhere safe?"

I nodded. "Come on. Let's try to find more. You can't survive on nothing but a few leaves."

At the end of the day we'd found four promising plants, including one with edible corms. "I think these are water chestnuts," Layla had said when she popped one in her mouth. I gazed at the pale corms until Layla shoved one in my mouth. The taste was mild and creamy, and left me wanting more.

Nothing like the food the Company made us eat.

We made our way back along the rows. How would we tell the others? How could we grow enough plants in secret to survive the Company's toxic meals?

We emerged from the rice paddy to a terrifying scene. The army truck was parked near the Wajbah. New refugees were being herded, at gunpoint, from wagons hitched to water buffalo. Company doctors waited to poke and prod us on our way into the Wajbah, taking blood, swabs, checking heads. Layla stiffened and every eye turned toward us.

"Get in line," a white-coated man said. We walked to the end of the line and stood, sweating, while I prayed they wouldn't discover my contraband plants or Layla's curse-mark.

Maybe it was gone?

A female doctor planted herself in front of me. "Open your mouth," she said, and I complied. Another doctor, quite young, arrived to check Layla. My heart raced, and when the doctor checked my blood pressure she made a small sound, then rechecked it.

"You must be stressed," she said, pulling the cuff off me. Black specks floated in front of my eyes—then I remembered to breathe.

The doctor stepped back and wrote 'Physically sound' on my file before she moved on. As I turned back to Layla I heard the junior doctor ask her to remove her headscarf.

The fieldworkers fell silent. With a trembling hand, Layla pulled the scarf from her head and turned around.

The bald patch on the back of her head revealed that the mark was still there. I moaned, covering my mouth with my hand.

The junior doctor swore and stepped back. "What the hell?"

I squinted at the mark; it was fainter than in the morning.

A hard-faced male doctor strode down the line and took hold of Layla's arm. "You'll have to come with us," he said.

"No!"

My skin crawled under the combined gazes of everyone present. I took a deep breath. "You do not understand," I said.

The senior doctor narrowed his eyes. "This is not your concern." He looked at Layla's file. "Layla will be safe while we conduct the tests."

The blood drained from my face. "No, she will not." I looked around at the others. Most of them avoided my gaze but a few stared at me with hostility. They were afraid of being cursed. "You have to help me," I said to them in Arabic.

Layla's face was pale. "It's all right," she said. The guards surrounded her and she was lost to my sight.

"No," I whispered. They loaded her into the truck with the doctors. It roared to life, and Layla was gone, leaving behind a cloud of exhaust smoke. The driver of the wagon swore and raised his rifle before whipping the water buffalos into action.

"What is wrong with you?" I cried in Arabic, turning on the others. "We found the cure! And now Layla has no chance!"

Frowns. Behrang, a burly Iranian man, stepped forward. "What are you saying? Speak in English so everyone can understand."

"The food. It is the food. Layla and I found some wild-growing plants and she was able to eat without dying. She should be dead, but she is not. Why did you not think?" My voice rose. "You should have helped!"

"What would you have had us do, Nasra? Our bare hands against their guns?"

I sank to the ground, a sob catching in my throat. The sack of contraband plants weighed heavily around my neck. Behrang reached out his calloused hand. I stared at it a moment, the tears blurring my vision, distorting his hand into a bulbous mass. Then I took it, and let him pull me up.

"I need to get to Layla."

"How?" An Islander woman strode forth, her wide shoulders thrown back as if to say *don't mess with me*. Her accent was thick, her English basic. "There a fence, there guards."

"I know." I thought about Abdul and Marhub. They were probably dead. There had to be a way out. "What if I pretended to have the mark?" I touched my head.

She leaned her head to the side. She nodded slightly, a small smile on her face. "And then what? If you right, by time they come back your sister will be already dead."

"Not if I take myself to the gate and beg for help."

Behrang and the Islander exchanged glances. "Yes," said Behrang. "We do this."

We barely touched the stew, eating as little as possible. "The sack I had today has edible plants in it," I said to Behrang. "Find somewhere to grow them. Stop killing the plants that grow wild."

Behrang mentioned Abdul's disappearance, followed by Mehmet's removal. "Perhaps, somehow, he reached New Venice, as he planned," I said, and Behrang looked thoughtful.

After dinner the Islander woman—whose name was Tangi—shaved some hair off the back of my head and mixed some rice flour and mud with water to create a sticky raised mess on my scalp. "Not look like face, but should be okay in the dark," she said. As it dried it felt itchy and tight on my shaved skin and I had to restrain myself from scratching at it.

I said my goodbyes and took the dirt road from the little worker's camp to the main gate of the croplands. There was enough moonlight to avoid potholes, though I turned my ankle on a rock. It twinged and throbbed, and I walked with a limp that became more pronounced the further I went.

Ahead the fence loomed. At the top rolls of barbed wire told me in no uncertain terms that we were prisoners. The fence bore a big sign in English that I couldn't read, but the symbol of lightning left me in no doubt what would happen should I touch the wire.

There was a small guardhouse outside the gate. A light shone dimly through the window. I approached the gate and started hollering. A man was silhouetted against the light, then he staggered out of the guardhouse and waved a rifle at me.

"Back away from the gate," he shouted. I raised my hands and backed up. He came closer, stopping a foot from the gate. "Go back."

"I am sick. The others will kill me. I need a doctor."

The guard, a young man of about twenty with a soft face and uncertain features, looked back at the guardhouse as though hoping someone else would come along and solve this problem for him.

I sat in the dirt and bowed my head. There was a long pause and then the gate swung open.

I glanced up from under the curtain of hair. The guard jerked his rifle. "Come forward," he said. I pushed myself up and walked through the open gate. As I neared him he backed away and aimed the rifle at me. "That way," he said and I walked over to the guardhouse. The gate swung shut behind me.

I was out.

"In the corner," he said and I went into the cramped little room. The guard got on the radio and swore into it for a few minutes. I could barely understand him. He stopped talking into the radio and stared at me. I leaned against the wall and dozed off, only to be woken by the stamp of hooves and creaking of axles. The buffalo-wagon had arrived. The guard went out and said more things in rapid English before yelling, "Come out! Nice and slow."

I eased through the doorway and smelled the thick water buffalo smell, of warm musty animal and earthy, cloying faeces. It made me want to throw up. The water buffalos—only six hitched to one wagon this time—snorted and tossed their heads, unhappy at being forced to work at this time of night.

"Up," the guard said, indicating to the empty wagon. The driver frowned at me.

"Get to the back, missy," he said, wrinkling his nose. "No funny business. If you try to run, I'll shoot you." He lifted his shotgun. I nodded.

My neck ached from nervous tension as I climbed into the wagon. The floor was littered with straw and smelled of composting matter. Limbs weary, I curled up in a corner and fell asleep.

As the sky crept toward dawn I woke, wrapped in the stench of the wagon and the bitterness of lantana. I caught a glimpse of the mists that smothered the canals of the Gold Coast. When we'd been transported to the Company paddy fields we learned the Gold Coast had become a maze of flooded streets that could only be travelled by boat. A consequence of global warming, as the sea reclaimed the land, the interpreter had said.

The wagon lumbered downhill. I lost sight of the eerie city as we entered a wasteland of abandoned houses and rotting roads. Cracked windows squinted in the murky light, doors hung off hinges, and here and there a wall crumbled, letting the invasive lantana vines penetrate the house.

"What is this place?" I asked.

The driver grunted. "It was called Pacific Pines, back before the world went to hell. The Company bought out the owners, evicted the tenants, turned it into a ghost suburb."

A bush turkey scurried into a broken house.

"Why?" I held my breath.

He turned and briefly looked at me. I gave him an encouraging smile.

"They wanted to keep the residents away," he said, his back facing me once more. I breathed out and kept my mouth shut. The water buffalos threw themselves against an uphill slope, straining, their bodies sweating with effort. As we crested the hill I saw stretched out below me a mass of lowset buildings, all uniform grey to reflect the pre-dawn sky. Fences even sturdier than the ones that trapped us in the paddy fields surrounded the complex. The sun broke free of the horizon, though our destination was still wrapped in shadows. I glanced back to the sunrise that turned the moody sea into liquid gold, before we began the final descent.

When Layla, Mama and I first boarded that boat for Australia, it was scary, but you could taste the hope. The waves lapped at the sides of the shabby boat as hundreds of desperate men, women and children crammed onto the deck. All I could smell was sweat, excrement and fear, seasoned by the salt in the air. So much could go wrong, but no-one wanted to stay and face the uncertainty of the refugee camps.

When the sun cleared the hill and bathed the complex in light, the view stole the last of my optimism. I crawled into my corner and shut my eyes.

The compound guard questioned the driver, and eventually the gates opened with a smooth hum. I breathed in the smell of straw and bit my cheek. Lights danced in the darkness behind my eyelids. The wagon jerked and began to roll forward. A different kind of vessel carried me into a future with no hope.

"Get up!"

I opened my eyes and squinted in the glare. Two men frowned at me from the other side of a Perspex wall. One was old, white, and dressed in a suit; the other middle-aged, south-east Asian, and dressed in a lab-coat marked with the Company's logo. Across from me an old orang-utan paced around its cell. I rolled to my knees and pushed myself up.

"You are Nasra?" the lab-coated man asked. "Egyptian national?"

I nodded.

"Why are you here?"

"I told you already." I swallowed, my tongue sticking to the roof of my mouth. "Can I have some water?"

"You do not have the mark."

"If I tell you what is causing the deaths," I stepped forward and put my hands against the Perspex barrier, "will you let me see my sister? Please?"

The old suited man stepped back and gestured to the lab-coated man, who opened the door to my cell. "Follow," the younger man said.

They took me down a short corridor pitted with clear barriers. Apathetic creatures and the occasional emaciated person ignored my passage. At the end of the hall the lab-coated man opened a heavy steel door and waited for me to enter.

The room was sterile, empty but for several stainless steel tables. The nearest to the door was covered in a white sheet. I looked around for Layla. "Where is my sister?"

The older man smiled. "You're looking at her." And he pointed at the covered table.

My skin went cold, my gut clenched. "No." I reached across and with a trembling hand lifted the sheet.

Layla's face was pale and still, her eyes fixed in a wide stare.

I fell to my knees, swallowing the bile that rose.

"Layla. Please, no."

The scientist dragged me to my feet. The Company man said, "You are to tell me what you know about the uprising. What connections do you have in New Venice?"

I blinked, clutching at my head. "I do not know what you are talking about."

Layla.

A sob shuddered through my body. The Company man stared at me then motioned the scientist to bring me. My vision blurred as I was hauled back to my cell and pushed in.

"This is not right," I said as I turned to face them. Tears welled. I swallowed the lump in my throat and forced them back. "We are not slaves. Not lab rats. We are people."

Through a wet haze I saw him regard me with eyes cold and hard as a bullet.

"Everything has a use. This is yours." The men turned to go.

"Wait! What did you mean by...uprising?"

The Company man paused and looked back over his shoulder. "You don't ask the questions. I'll be back in a few hours. We may as well find a use for you now you're here."

The orang-utan scratched her head and watched me with dead eyes. I backed away from the barrier and sat with my back to the cold wall.

Uprising. Revolution.

I closed my eyes and smelled smoke and tear gas, dust and fear. A fierce heat burned inside me. We refugees were no strangers to revolution. They could use me in their science experiments. They had given me the hope I needed to hold on.

DELIVER ME

J.S. Choinski

The oars sliced into the water. Straining, he leant forward, willing them to rise out of the water and propel the boat forward.

A mozzie had found its way underneath his damp collar and began to bite. If he let go to shoo it away, the oars might slide into the brown water. Then he would have to get out of the little rowboat into the stinking morass and dive until he found them. It wasn't the mud, stench or shivering in the boat afterwards that made him avoid water: it was the Things.

He thought one of the Things had grasped his ankle the last time he had gone into the water. Or maybe it was just a root. He hadn't stayed to find out. Every time he thought of stopping, just stopping, letting everything slide from his hands, lying back into the boat and letting them take him—he'd hear one. Slightly, just above the din of the cicadas and wading bird's cries, he'd hear a moan.

Lucky, he thought, shivering and momentarily displacing the mosquito.

That's what I am—real lucky. Threw a seven and here I am.

He ignored the stinging bite of the mosquito and found the strength to row on.

The water began to move. There was a current, sucking him forward to his destination. He turned around to glance at the sack at the front of the boat. Where once the sack had lain flat, now it bulged surreptitiously with unknown goods. His stomach lurched.

What had that poncy bloke said that actors say? Oh, right, he thought. "Break a leg," he whispered to himself. He was *on*.

The boat was moving faster, the mangroves a blur. He brought the oars back into the boat and hugged them to his chest. There was a loud cracking noise. He squeezed his eyes shut. He'd know when he needed to start rowing again.

After some time, (Minutes? Years?), the wind stopped stinging his face and the boat began to slow. Mercifully, it wasn't raining. He opened his eyes and saw that the current was strong, but nothing he couldn't manage. The boat scraped over something metal. There was an excited yelp from behind him. He twisted around in the boat to look at what had made the noise.

A sunburnt boy was perched on what must have been a roof. The thick water had swallowed up the rest of the house. Plastic debris floated around, being pulled into the little whirlpools. Only the very tops of the trees emerged from the stinking floodwater.

The boy had a towel draped on his head—a feeble attempt to lessen the damage of the sun. In his arms was a small mutt, squirming to get away and yipping excitedly.

In the distance the man could see Mt Warning. He couldn't see any other man-made structures or anything else to give him a clue as to what suburb he was in—all he knew was that he was in the Hinterland, far, far away from the beloved beaches and sparkling oceans of his youth.

The ocean…can I ever see it again? No, no, no. Can't think of that. Focus. Focus.

He slid the oars back into the water and heaved the boat forwards until he drew level with the boy. The boy looked at him warily.

"My name's Jack," the lie came easily to the man. It was better that no-one knew the truth. "Where's your parents at?" he asked, trying to sound casual.

"Away. At a wedding," she said, peering from beneath the towel.

It seems that the boy was, in fact, a girl. Jack was old-fashioned enough to disapprove of women wearing pants. Girls ought to act like girls. He couldn't imagine why her parents hadn't taught her that.

"Your parents left you all alone?" he asked.

"Nah," she said, warming up a little. "My brother and sister were here, too, but they went out for pizza and DVDs while it was raining. Guess they got cut off by the flood." She shrugged, as if the absence of her siblings made no difference, but Jack could see the fear in her eyes. Even though she was scared, the girl met his gaze unflinchingly. They were blue, like the way he remembered the ocean.

Pizza…DVDs…? No, not worth asking. Just get the job done right, Jack thought.

The dog made another lunge for freedom, but the girl held tight.

Yip, yip, yip. Jack didn't approve of pets either. Animals should have a purpose to them. He could understand the point of proper dogs—dogs that could chase cattle, protect your family or kill a rat—but this dirty little thing was a waste. He'd best make an effort, though, as he still had to get her into the boat.

"What's the little beggar's name?" he asked.

She hesitated. She was probably remembering admonishments to not trust strangers.

You shouldn't, Jack thought. *Except this once. Trust me; trust a stranger just this time. Please.*

He didn't want to have to force her into the boat. That would make things more difficult.

The dog finally worked its way free of her grasp and leapt into the boat. Jack cringed backwards, holding up the oar to fend off the dog as it leapt at his face, trying to lick him. She laughed.

"He's Dough and mine's Jane," she said.

Liar, he thought.

Her name didn't matter, so he let it pass.

"Nice to meet you, Jane. If you're not busy, maybe I can take you and Dough somewhere a bit safer to wait for your family?" he said.

Jane had already slid into the boat before he had finished talking and used her towel to wrap Dough up and stop him from bothering Jack.

She began to prod the sack. "What's in here?" she asked.

Jack shrugged and pushed the boat away from the roof. He looked around, trying to see if there was any obvious direction he should head in, but there was nothing but murky water and bits of trees in sight.

Jane pulled out something covered in plastic from the sack. She unwrapped it and sniffed at it surreptitiously. "Ugh, cheese and Vegemite. How old is this sandwich?"

Jack shrugged again, starting to row away from the house.

She crammed the sandwich into her mouth and as she chewed she said, "It's stale. You're lucky I'm starving."

Dough wagged his tail.

Jane reached into the sack again. "You've got dog biscuits?" she asked, incredulously.

He was glad he wasn't facing her as he shrugged again and thought: *Christ. I better take care of the bloody dog then.*

The current began to pick up again.

He shouted over his shoulder, "Get down into the boat and hold Dough tight. It's about to get real rough."

The boat didn't slow down this time, but it began to rain. It never rained in the other place, the place of waiting, so Jack knew they had arrived at their next destination. Jane found a tarp in the sack, stretched it out over part of the boat and huddled underneath in an attempt to stay dry. She looked scared, but said nothing.

Jack wanted to say, "It'll be all right," but he was too busy trying to steer the boat to avoid smashing into a gum tree and bailing it out as it filled up with rain. Besides, too many times before it hadn't been all right. Some things he couldn't lie about.

"Here! Over here!"

Jack swiveled. There was a young man in a suit atop a white car that was slowly moving along with the water. He was waving a little black rectangle around.

Please let it not be a weapon, thought Jack as he maneuvered the boat towards the car. The young man began to scream as an exhausted black snake slithered onto the car's roof.

"It'll be all right," Jack said wryly, as he helped the young man into the boat.

For the snake. That's at least too right. The poor bugger, Jack thought. Nature could always be relied upon to throw a six-and-a-half, unlike us.

"SES, right? Christ, you guys sure get here quick. Name's Lachlan." As the young man sat down, the boat enlarged to accommodate him. Jane's eyes widened, but Lachlan didn't seem to notice.

"Actually didn't think you'd be able to find me. Thought my call had gotten cut off before I told you where I was," he waggled the black rectangle in Jack's face.

Ah, thought Jack, *not a weapon. Just a phone.*

Lachlan continued, looking at his car: "Bloody dealership. Supposed to be an all-terrain four wheel drive. Had to go do some surveying for the council, drove through a bloody puddle and here I am. Thank Christ you came along. I'll be sure to drop some money next time you guys shake the tin."

Jack nodded and pushed the boat away from the car. They were swept away into the torrents of floodwater.

"Mate, I don't want to tell you your business, but shouldn't we be heading here?" asked Lachlan, gesturing upstream and then showed Jack something on his phone, tapping insistently.

God, thought Jack, *surveying. For the council. Just like me. Or like I was.* He looked into Lachlan's untroubled eyes. *Was I ever that young, that confident, that arrogant?* He grimaced. *Probably worse. Don't make the same mistake I did, kid.*

Out loud he said, "Sorry, *mate,* but I can't row against the current. And there's someone else who we've got to pick up." He sensed that was true, as the rowboat began to speed faster than the water was carrying them.

Lachlan reluctantly settled deep into the boat. Jane handed him the sack without a word. He thrust his hand into it and withdrew a thermos.

"Cappuccino? Shit, you guys think of everything, don't you? Cheers mate!" Lachlan mock toasted.

Jack nodded, as they were carried into the night.

There was another loud cracking noise.

Jane recoiled, Dough howled and Lachlan yelled, "Christ, what was that?!"

Wait, no, that's not right —

Where are we now?

It was too dark to see anything but darker voluminous shapes. Lachlan held up his phone and with its light they caught glimpses of the objects they floated past: ghostly gum trees, rusty car, parts of fences...no-one said anything—not even Dough. The sloshing of the oars seemed to be an intrusion into the hushed silence.

Jack squinted and looked up. Only some of the stars were visible, but they were arranged in a comfortably familiar pattern. There were no moans, either.

We're not in the other place then. Still somewhere in the hinterland. Must be time for another pick-up —

"Coo-eee! Hello?" yelled Jack. His cry didn't echo into the night, but was instead absorbed by it. Then there was a silence, as if the night was considering its reply.

"– here. I'm right here," a faint but unmistakable cry came from their left.

As Jack maneuvered the craft towards the origin of the cry, Lachlan began to tap on his phone again, muttering "Bloody GPS isn't working." Jack could only grunt in return, using all his concentration to steer the boat.

"I'm right here." A hand snaked out of the darkness and grabbed

Jack by the arm.

"Jesus!" Lachlan exclaimed. Startled, he dropped his phone in the boat.

Once he had retrieved it, they were able to see an elderly lady serenely sitting in the top of a eucalyptus, the tips of her feet dangling in the water.

"What are you doing up there?" Lachlan demanded.

"Waiting for you," she said dryly. "Now boys, I may have gotten myself up here, but I'm going to need your help getting down. And before we get intimate, I think we should introduce ourselves—you may call me Mrs Lees."

"Jack," he said, reaching to tug at his hat, before realizing that he no longer wore one.

Lachlan held out his hand to shake. She leant forward across the gap between the tree and the boat and managed to grasp the tips of his fingers. "Maroney, Lachlan. With the council," he introduced himself.

"I'm Jane and this is Dough." Dough wagged his stumpy tail enthusiastically. Mrs Lees gave a fond smile.

"Mrs Lees, is your husband around? Or anyone else?" Lachlan asked.

"No. No-one lives here anymore." Mrs Lees turned and gave Jack a brief piercing glare. *Her eyes...so familiar...*

"I'm sure our Mayor would be sorry to hear that," Lachlan said. To Jack, he tapped his head and mouthed "ga-ga".

She doesn't look soft—but what was she doing up in a tree? No, no, doesn't matter. Just get her out and on her way. Hope she doesn't break a hip. Or, thinking of earlier, *a leg.*

It took all three of them to transfer her to the boat. Jack and Lachlan lifted her out of the tree, while Jane struggled to keep the boat still with one of the oars.

Strong little thing, Jack approved.

He may have only been a paper-pusher in his former life, but he had since learnt to appreciate strength. Dough helped out by yapping loudly and generally getting in the way. Once again the boat enlarged to fit Mrs Lees, but Lachlan didn't notice and Jane seemed too tired to care.

As Mrs Lees settled in, Jack let the boat drift with the swift current. Lachlan tapped at his phone again. The dog began to intensely smell Mrs Lees leg and then started to lick her foot.

"Stop that, Lucky," Mrs Lees commanded. He obeyed with a little wag of the tail.

Jane looked up, surprised and suspicious. "How did you know his name was Lucky?" she demanded.

"Oh," she replied scratching Lucky on the head, "he looked like he should be named Lucky. Now my dear, I didn't quite catch your name before...?"

"Rhea," said the girl formerly known as Jane. She gave Jack a guilty glance, but he pretended to be busy with the oars. *Knew it. Knew she was lying –*

Again, there was a thundering crack. Everyone on the boat winced and Lucky moaned. It was suddenly light enough to see.

Is the sun setting or rising? I can never tell.

The floodwaters had evidently subsided and they were on a proper waterway—*probably the Nerang River*, Jack thought.

"Hey, the GPS is working again!" Lachlan exclaimed, pleased with himself and gesturing to his phone.

As they floated along, some buildings came into view.

Finally. Houses? Shops? Doesn't matter.

Jack steered the boat to a shallow embankment.

"Is this where the SES have set-up?" Lachlan asked. Jack nodded, lying. Lachlan clambered out of the boat and helped Rhea out.

Now for the tricky bit, thought Jack.

"Jack, would you mind rowing me a little further along? I'm a little too old to be walking that far…" Mrs Lees asked.

Relieved, Jack nodded. He gave a little wave and pushed the boat down the river. Lachlan scrambled up the embankment, but Rhea remained, watching the boat intensely. Lucky howled mournfully. Jack grimaced.

"Now, don't you be worrying about her. She'll be fine. They'll both be fine," Mrs Lees said.

Jack nodded, only half listening.

"She won't forget you either, she –"

There was again, a loud crack. They were no longer on the river, but *a canal maybe…? Where are we?* Jack looked around. There were remains of buildings on either side of them, too large to be houses. Water filled their ground floors.

Ignoring the jarring transition, Mrs Lees continued, "– she thinks you're some kind of Santa, what with that sack of yours."

She paused. They both looked at an avenue of large, dead palm trees as they drifted past. She then turned back to Jack and continued, the words pouring out of her.

"She keeps on looking for you everywhere and she finds a repeated story of a man—in newspapers, on the web, on TV, on microfiche—a man who calls himself Jack and rescues people in a row-boat during floods on the Gold Coast and disappears, never aging, never appearing under any other circumstance, over the last hundred years –"

They glided past a building with the image of a large guitar. Only part of the sign remained 'The…Rock Ca…'. Another building they floated past was pink and its sign had been defaced to read 'The Pink Puddle'. Jack watched passively, letting Mrs Lees' monologue wash over him.

"– so then she thought you were an angel, Jack, a guardian angel.

But then she found a photo, a photo of you as a council employee –"

Jack caught sight of something strange between the buildings.

It was blue.

What, no, it couldn't, it couldn't be—the...ocean?

"Jack," said Mrs Lees laying her hand on his arm to get his attention. "Jack, she—I know who you are. I know your real name. And I know what you did."

Jack stared at her, transfixed. "You said it was safe. All those people who died, who lost their homes, their property in the floods. They developed those places on the Gold Coast because you said it was safe. And after you died, you had to –"

"Yes." Though his mouth had gone dry, he managed to choke the admission out.

To atone. To repent. To be delivered from evil.

"I didn't realise, until a couple of years ago when I looked into the mirror, that *I* was her. The old lady." She laughed. "Then of course, it made sense why she didn't get out of the boat and I never saw her again."

"Rhea." Jack said. That's why her eyes were so familiar.

She smiled. "It was such a treat to see Lucky again. I cried so much when he passed away. And of course once I realized that I was Mrs Lees, I knew what I had to do."

"Do what –?" Jack asked.

"Jack, look around you! This is Surfer's Paradise. Now, I know you wouldn't have heard of climate change, but it must be obvious that there's no-one else here. I meant it when I said no-one lives here anymore—no-one lives anywhere on the Gold Coast anymore. We can't."

She leant forward and gripped his hands so hard, that he could no longer hold onto the oars. "I –" Jack began.

"I'm here to tell you that it's over." Rhea squeezed his hands.

"There's no-one here to rescue. You are forgiven."

Jack looked into Rhea's eyes, the abandoned buildings and the blue, blue ocean.

He began to weep.

DUCK

Jane Downing

4

It was always hot in the car. That was Mel's main memory of Christmas. Even the years they had to go through floods and she or one of the others had to get out to walk in front of the car. If the water got above their thighs the car wasn't going to make it across the ford, but somehow they always got there, finally driving into town, passing under the railway bridge. "Duck," Dad would say, and Mel would dip her head into the vinyl of the backseat so she wouldn't bump it on the brick underside of the bridge. He kept saying it, Christmas after Christmas, even when they were too old to think this a likely help, or to think it funny, or to think anything after all the hours in the heat in the backseat, squabbling over whose turn it was to sit in the middle and who got a window so they could look out at all the trees.

Trees, everywhere they looked, now they were far from the city. But in the lounge at their grandparents' place the Christmas tree was as synthetic as 1970s fashions. Plastic silver leaves; snow hinted in the tinsel glint. Snow like the stuff on the Christmas cards hanging like washing from lines strung around the house. Cards from people who only existed in black and white behind pictures of red-breasted robins and angel choirs; from aunties and uncles too far removed by geography to be part of the gathering due to arrive throughout Christmas morning.

In they'd go, hugs and kisses and a rush off to the toilet down the backstairs of the old Queenslander, wondering what they could read on the 'loo paper,' local news or something more glossy and risqué. Stuff good for the sitting but not always so good for the ending up…

"Not that it's anything like that now." Mel was stopped in the full flight of her remembrances with a steely bullet of reality. She was taking her boyfriend to a family Christmas. For the first time. She didn't want to put Hiroshi off.

She glanced across at him in the driver's seat. He was squinting slightly under his sunglasses. It would have made more sense for her to drive. She knew the roads from all those Christmases—but she'd instinctively known she had to give him some control over the situation. There was no way she'd have agreed to fronting up to his family en masse in Kyoto. She worried she'd badgered him into the trek up the highway, but he had to meet her family sometime. She couldn't keep worrying about Pop's reaction.

His long gentle hands moved left over right to turn a corner. The bridge was in sight. "Duck?" he said.

Mel wanted to leap across into his arms. They'd smash into the bridge abutment but she'd die happy.

"I'm sure there's been an improvement in toilet paper since Mum and Dad moved back last winter to look after Pop. No more cut-down newspaper. All bleached white soft and lab-tested now."

Mel checked the rear-vision mirror, and chided herself.

Lab-tested? What am I thinking?

Hiroshi worked in a lab. One day he might cure cancer and here she was belittling labs with talk of toilet paper texture. She was about to go into a confusing description of Labrador puppies pulling rolls of the paper across smart green lawns like in the ad, except that would only confirm that she was trivial.

Mel, shut up, she told herself. The silence grew to fill the car.

Mel wound the window down a bit, to see if she could smell the eucalypts.

"In Japan we are ridiculous about Christmas," Hiroshi said, now they were on the straight heading into town. "Last year in our prefecture someone decided to decorate for the season. Santa Claus was crucified in a window."

Last year Hiroshi was looking at a crucified Santa.

Surely my family can't be any worse than that.

3

Derek heard the muted gunshot crunch of a car coming up the driveway. More relatives most likely. "Four generations," his Dad had said as they'd pulled in the day before. Four generations, as if that was something special. Derek's best friend was going to Magnetic Island with just his mum and dad. If you had to come to Queensland for Christmas, that was the way to do it.

There were busy noises bustling from the house above him. A radio crooning, a fan squealing at one point in each rotation, the muted chatter of little-girl cousins living in a Barbie world; an electric beater whipping egg whites or cream: a sound that promised pavlova for dessert.

Gran, with a floured-apron tying her into two bulging pillows of fat, never stopped moving even when there were aunties—daughters, nieces, cousins—around to help. The uncles—brothers, nephews, cousins—were helping by being out of the way.

An hour before, Derek's father had announced they were off "hunting and fishing." Derek figured that meant buying fresh prawns from the van in the car park on the beachfront and stopping at the pub on the way back.

Derek wasn't quite a man yet; he was sent out the back so as not to be underfoot. With limbs growing long and not quite fitting, and a voice as ungainly, and hair growing in nameless dark places, Derek was always in the way, even of Derek.

The washing machine knocked to a halt under the house. His mother's flip-flops slapped down the backstairs. She dragged the washing trolley into the darkness of the under-house after her.

A passionfruit vine sprawled over the trellis between the stumps so it was almost as if this area under the house was walled in. Only one part actually was—the part over on the right behind the downstairs' toilet. This was his great-grandfather's workshop. Emanations of mystery and dread seeped out from that side. He was called Pop the Headhunter, though not within his hearing. Something to do with the war. And headhunting. Obviously.

A flock of birds swooped over the back fence. Derek cocked an ear and tuned out of this station, which his mother fondly called reality, because this was just such a scenario that would be on the screen before the Apocalypse. Life going on, no warning, and then *boom*.

There'd be a Secret Government Facility nearby, complete with advanced technologies hidden underground. The enemy strike would take out the pilots so of course Derek, as the only teenage boy around—as the plot always went in his favourite anime—would have to step in, and step up, to get one of the Gundam fighting robots into the air.

A bevy of gorgeous female technicians would help him into the cockpit and he'd sit in the chest cavity: a beating heart in the ten-metre tall mechanical robot. His hands would settle onto the controls. Recognise them instinctively. Up they'd fly into the blue.

"Pick some passionfruit for the pav would you?" Derek's mum asked as she pushed past with the mound of wet clothes. He caught a glimpse of a commodious bra at the peak, and embarrassed, turned away.

Talk about being brought back to earth.

"Ten, maybe twelve," his mum called back from the Hills Hoist.

Derek, obedient for now, went closer to the house. He stretched his hand into the mass of leaves, letting his fingers search out the fossilised scrotums of fruit that had somehow got the name passion attached to them. He snapped one from its branch, imagining his fingers were Gundam giant and the stalks were the bones of his enemy.

A clang of metal falling on cement under the house delivered him back to Christmas again. He wasn't allowed to load any anime on his laptop this holiday. Nothing Japanese was allowed in the house— because of Pop's war. Last century.

Pop, lurking in there.

Derek's parents had speculated in the car, somewhere around the state border when they thought he was listening to his iPod or asleep, that Pop had lost it. He wasn't pottering in his workshop, he was simply potty. Derek imagined he could smell eau de old man from where he stood, though it was more likely the struggling septic tank.

So he quickly snapped seven passionfruit and chucked them in the laundry basket on top of the last wet towels.

"Hey," his mum called. But anime heroes don't listen to their mums. Their parents are conveniently dead. Derek kept running around the side of the house.

The latest car to arrive was in front of the house with the boot up. A blond head bobbed into view. Aunty Mel. She propped a backpack against the iris-borders, dipped back behind the shield of the boot, and laughed at something. Two laughs blended. The boot lid slammed down revealing Hiroshi, the fellow-laugher.

Derek had watched so much anime over the last year that he felt as if he understood the language. He wanted to greet the stranger in Japanese. But all he could get out was, "*Sugoi.*" Great. *Sugoi*, meaning great. No matter what the older generation thought about his generation, he wasn't being ironic.

2

Stan had a peephole through the wooden fretwork that laced between the house stumps. The bougainvillea ran unchecked at the front and it coloured the shadows green. Sometimes he forgot if he was in the jungles of Borneo or stuck under the house with memories.

It was quiet under there, now the washing machine was done, and some woman had pushed out the trolley he'd made from a crate and four obsolete pram wheels. Now all the noise was outside with the new arrivals: a silver car, Korean make, not much better than Japanese. Stan's fingers grabbed the fretwork as a lanky figure uncurled itself from behind the wheel. A sharp sword of bougainvillea thorn pierced Stan's knuckle. He drew back and sucked the blood.

He would have paid a good five Dutch Gilders for that head. The Dyaks were happy with the money and the authorities didn't ask too many questions. He still had a blowpipe in his steamer trunk: one poison dart and it'd all be over.

Stan bent forward and peered out again. Brazen, full light of day, sacred time of year, and here was the invader with a laughing face on. No smiles on the heads he bought to save his country from invasion.

Did that Jap intend to come into his house? He was lifting a suitcase out of the compact Korean boot. He was kicking Stan's gravel with a polished black boot. He stepped closer. Stan couldn't watch. He pushed back into the sawdusty smell of his workshop. The steamer trunk was in here somewhere, under seventy years of sawdust and normal dust—the accumulation of shed human skin.

The trunk was buried by time, unlike the memories which had travelled with him, playing like a cinema reel in the back of his mind as his family gathered around the table for dinner, and the minister blessed the holy sacrament on Sundays, and the lawn mower hacked the grass under the Hills Hoist, and his son showed him his cricket final's trophy, and his wife said *let's go to bed* and held him when he couldn't do what husbands are supposed to do because he wasn't a husband or a father or a house owner or parishioner or civilised man; he was a soldier in a jungle asking headhunters to kill his enemy and counting out foreign coin for the severed heads he carried away in a bag over his shoulder.

Stan found the key in a jar of loose nails and screws. He steadied one hand next to the vise before lowering himself onto his knees below his workbench. The trunk was covered by an old bath mat his wife couldn't throw out.

The key ground its way into the padlock, rust against rust, orange star motes of it peppering his hand. The lid had no room to fully lift under the confines of the bench so he wedged his left shoulder in to keep it from snapping shut again. It was all shadows inside. His knees ached on the cement.

The washing trolley squealed up the path and each clunking rotation of the wheels echoed under the house. Stan ignored the jolly 'Jingle Bells' ditty his granddaughter hummed, though it reminded him of the whistling amongst the troops: the small noises on the long marches to keep the mayhem at bay. He let his hand walk through the layers in the trunk.

Souvenirs jostled out of the way. The small tin Betty had sent him with a slice of fruit cake, Christmas 1942; the Dyak blowpipe and the old service gun his guide called a *snapbang*. Letters, a ration book, loose photographs he couldn't give Betty for the family albums, and at the bottom…the sword. In the shadows, his fingers read the raised pattern on the hilt and stroked along the scabbard, leathery like his own skin.

The Samurai sword had cost him more than a handful of Dutch Gilders.

1

Pammy had grandchildren of her own playing in the lounge room and backyard, yet she still felt like a usurper banging about in her mother's kitchen. A woman's kitchen was her castle and, ten years after her death, her mother's reign lingered.

No wonder Pop called out, "Betty, Betty, is that you putting the kettle on?" His age wasn't robbing him of the certainty of where he was so much as *when* he was. The look on his face when he realised it was only his daughter: like he was being hit with the first fist of grief again.

"These potatoes won't peel themselves," Pammy called. Footsteps bounced on the floorboards of the closed-in verandah, then any hope of help headed in the opposite direction.

A screen door slammed. A "hello" whooped.

Pammy jiggled the ties of her apron and hung the gingham square across the bench top, smoothed her dress across her rolls and her hair against her skull, leaving trails of flour and traces of castor sugar, but feeling the better for greeting the new arrivals.

She stopped at the linen closet to grab a couple of towels and counted again in her head the beds, trundles and mattresses on the floor and mulled over the delicate matter of whether Mel and her new boyfriend should be in the same room, and whose sensibilities were at risk.

Her husband's car turned into the drive as she finally came down the front stairs calling, "The kettle's on! Come on up, give me a kiss, beautiful girl," and all the other spoken chords of love. Everyone was here at last. The men were in the driveway, the prawns could be peeled, head off, tail, guts.

Young Derek stampeded around the corner to join the melee— shoulders thrusting, legs wide—like he was Godzilla or had poo in his pants. Hiroshi stood to one side when the hugging started. Pammy reached out a hand to include him. She held his arm lightly so he couldn't stray too far from the fold, but her eyes were on Mel, all soft and vulnerable looking behind big sunglasses. She knew she had to be politically correct here; this young man was nothing like any of the others Mel had brought home.

Pammy didn't see Pop emerge from under the house. Hiroshi's arm slipped out of her grasp. She turned and her father was there.

She'd tried not to see this coming: her father's reaction to a Japanese man on his doorstep. "Pop, no," she called. Too late.

He thrust his arms at Hiroshi. The second car braked behind Mel's. Pammy didn't have enough arms to hold and bind but Mel pushed forward and young Derek appeared, suddenly a shield. Pammy, her daughter, her grandson, Pop: four generations in front of the house, in still life.

When Pop turned and hobbled away, even the birds in the trees were silent.

Hiroshi was pale. He was holding something. He slowly turned the photo so Pammy and Mel could see the figures caught in the small dog-eared square. A souvenir any soldier had in his pocket. Something to take out in the jungle to soothe him, to explain why he was fighting.

The woman wears a kimono of light cloth. The *obi* sash is darker, black to its white, in the photograph. The Japanese soldier's two children stand beside his wife, the girl holding her hand, the boy a step back, his hand a blur as it brushes the branch of a flowering bush.

Pammy is certain the love in their eyes is for their father behind the camera.

DEAR SAM

Jocelyn Hawes

Numinbah Valley
5ᵗʰ August, 1942

Dear Sam,

Your Dad said I should write you a letter. He's not one for using a pen and paper as you know. He said to tell you that we have a new lad working on the farm now. One of the Murphy boys, Clive—a big strong boy of thirteen. He left school in July when he had his birthday. He desperately wants to join up. His mother is glad that he can't. Two of his brothers were captured when Singapore fell earlier this year. Bertha Murphy longs to hear from them but even the Red Cross can't find any trace of them. Sad days.

We got your letter. It came via somewhere in New South Wales. We were glad to get the bits that the censor did not cut out. The camp sounds a grim place to be. The fruitcake we sent you must have got lost on the way. I hope the thief enjoyed it.

Katie has joined the Junior Red Cross and is knitting you a washer. She is learning not to drop stitches now and it looks passable if a bit lopsided. We still have dances at the hall run by the Comforts Fund and we do a lot of cooking so we can provide a nice supper. I know your mouth will water just thinking of all the cakes and biscuits. Oh my dear Sam, I do wish you could come back soon.

So sorry about the ink blots on the paper. The paper is so thin and tears easily. The ink is mixed with my tears. We are all being so brave but sometimes we aren't.

Bill usually knows when I'm really down and he follows me up the hill to the rock and we sit there and watch the sun go down. He's a good mate. After you left he was so restless at night. After years of sleeping on your bed I think, so I put an old jumper of yours in the basket near the stove and that comforted him.

Last week was your twenty-second birthday so we took a picnic and trudged up the hill to the Arch and swam in the water under the falls. It was cold despite the sunshine. Then we sat around and yarned until the sun went down and the glow-worms came out to shine for us. They were like a million little candles. We talked about you and told jokes.

I am running out of paper now so I must close but you would be interested to know that some evacuees have come to the valley, mainly mothers with young children from Brisbane. Most of the men have joined up or are in essential services like your Uncle Jack.

We will bake you another cake and hope it reaches you.

Goodnight my own dear son. May God Bless and keep you safe.

Your loving mother.

Somewhere in the Middle East
September, 1942

Dear Mother and Dad and my special sister, Katie,
Your letter arrived. I meant to ask you how Gran was these days. You did not mention her or Pop in your last letter. Please thank Katie for the washer. Such a nice green colour. Your cake arrived a bit squashed but was gratefully received by all my mates. A change from hard dry biscuits. I cannot tell you where we are but at present things are fairly quiet here. It is also very hot and dry.

Hope Clive is enjoying the milking. I remember him being just a little nipper when I was at school with his older brother, George. Is Miss Blake still at the school?

So many people have lost so much. It's no different here. Families destroyed and homes wrecked. The world may never be the same again. I long to be in the valley again and hear the laughter of the kookas and even an odd crow or two would be welcome. I even miss getting up to milk the cows at dawn.

I have a lot of good mates here and we look out for one another. The boss, as we call our sergeant is fair most times but has a hell of a temper when roused. Reminds me of Uncle Jack when he stood on the red-bellied black that time when we were coming back from the Arch and Katie had slipped over in the cow pat. It is those memories that keep me going.

Please keep on writing even if I don't answer as often as I'd like to. Stay safe. Love to everyone. Please give Bill an extra pat from me.
Your loving son,
Sam.

Numinbah Valley
September, 1942

Dear Sam,

We've had early storms this year and getting the milk truck in has been hard. It got stuck on the causeway and old Jonesy had to drag it off with his tractor. Your Dad hurt his back when he slipped in the mud. But it is healing well. Katie was overjoyed to hear that you received the washer. She is busy knitting you a scarf now in red, white and blue wool. We unravelled an old jumper to get enough wool.

You might be interested to know that Eleanor was home on leave recently. She looks very smart in her new uniform. She says she is heading north to work in Townsville as the hospitals there are getting wounded soldiers from New Guinea now. She read your letter and sends her love to you. Such a pretty girl but so determined to do good and help out. Her parents worry about her.

Gran and Pop are well too. They are both getting older but are glad the winter is over as Pop's lumbago gets worse in the cold months. They came up for visit recently. Pop was sorry that it was so wet as he wanted to climb up to the Arch. They are billeting some men who are working in essential services at the aerodrome. Accommodation is hard to find in the city.

We made a fuss of Bill and gave him a great big bone. His tail didn't stop wagging. Katie took a photo of him with the Brownie box camera which Pop lent her. If we can get it developed we'll send it to you, in the meantime I've drawn a small picture for you of our house. Dad thinks I am silly to be so sentimental. I'm running out of space again. Hope this letter arrives safely. Dear Sam, we think of you every day.

Your loving mother.

P.S. Another cake is on its way with the photo and my drawing. Hope you get them.

Middle East
September, 1942

Dear Mum, Dad and Katie,

Played cricket today with my mates. So hot in the sun but our team won. Then it was drinks all round. A change from being in the trenches. I can't say much here but I believe we are moving out soon. Don't know where or when. Let's hope we'll be closer to home. We don't really know what is happening.

Glad you saw Eleanor again. She always was a great girl. She loved to play tricks on George and I when we were all at school together. So long ago.

No letters from you lately. But I know you think of us and even thinking about you all brings you closer.

Must catch the post with this one.

Sam.

Numinbah Valley
October, 1942

Dear Sam,

Another month has gone by and we still haven't heard from you. I know that mail is slow and that you are so far away. Katie says to tell you that she is learning to cook scones so that when you come home she'll be able to make a batch for you.

I've been collecting dandelions and drying them for tea. I use wild honey to sweeten it. There are many food shortages here now but we are fortunate to be able to grow our own vegetables and the chooks are laying well.

Gran came up for a few days and we made jam from the strawberries and pickled some onions. Your Dad's favourite. Some of the younger children from the school came with Miss Blake to see the new calves. So life in the valley goes on as we wait to hear from you. I pray every night for you and your mates.

Please write soon.

Your loving mother.

Kokoda Track, New Guinea
November, 1942

Dear Mother and Dad,

Things are really bad here. This may be my last letter. Just remember that...and think of me often. The gunfire is getting closer. Must get my rifle and move under cover.

Thank God the jungle is thick here.

xx Sam.

Numinbah Valley
November, 1942

Dear Sam,

We haven't heard from you lately and hope all is well. Dad said you might be coming down under again as he heard on the wireless that some troops have moved into the Owen Stanley ranges and are fighting on the Kokoda track. The Murphys heard yesterday that their eldest son, Blue, was a prisoner-of-war in Japan. They are heartbroken but at least they think he may still be alive. They haven't heard anything about George yet. So we have crossed our fingers and we pray hard that no news is good news.

I'm so sorry to tell you but I wake crying every night. Terrible nightmares. We are trying so hard to be brave.

We had a letter from Eleanor. She has volunteered to go to Port Moresby to work in the field hospital there. Katie has finished her scarf. It's a bit crooked. She's going to keep it and give it to you when you come home.

It's early summer here and the wildflowers are blooming in the bush. We even saw the King orchid flowering up near the falls. Dad has delivered two more calves. We had to hand feed them for a few weeks but they are fine now.

I pray that we will hear from you soon our darling son,

From,

Your loving family. Mum, Dad, Katie, Gran and Pop and Bill.

Numinbah Valley
December, 1942

Dear Sam,

At last, news of you came in an official telegram from the Army. We were too scared to open it in case it was the worst possible news. Dad's hands shook as he slit the envelope open and then we read that you were alive but badly wounded in action in New Guinea. So close to home and yet so far away.

We heard more news from the Army letter that came later. How you were treated by doctors at the field hospital in Port Moresby and that you would be flown back to Australia as soon as you were well enough.

We hope that Eleanor may have nursed you. It is always wonderful to see a familiar face when one is suffering.

There are no words, dear son, for the relief that we all feel here. That you are safe and will soon be home again. Now we can all celebrate Christmas with joy in our hearts.

We long to see you. So much to tell you. Hurry home.

Your loving mother.

Greenslopes Hospital, Brisbane

January, 1943

Dear Mum and Dad and everyone else,

Good news. I'm back home in Australia—in Brisbane not far from you all. My wound is healing thanks to the good care of Eleanor and other nurses who looked after me in Moresby.

I was carried out of the jungle by four strong Papuans called the Fuzzy Wuzzy Angels. It was a rough ride down the track. It took forever.

Hopefully I'll be discharged soon and I can come home to the valley. Please come to see me soon. I need you.

Love to all the family,

Sam.

WAR BRIDE

Kay Gibb

The rocks are rough beneath my hands as I lean back and turn my face towards the sun, longing to feel its warmth radiate through me, as it once did. There's been some rain, so the air is moist and the waterfall in full flow. Other than the sounds of nature, the air is quiet. It's still too early for the families who like to come here to picnic, so for now I will enjoy this place in solitude. Springbrook has to be my favourite place on earth, but also the saddest.

James and I came here on our first date. He'd been coming into Dad's milk bar for weeks, buying the odd lolly here, chewing gum there—stuff he didn't need. I knew he was just looking for excuses to see me. In a town full of American soldiers with nothing but time on their hands, we local girls were used to it. But there was something different about James. He was humble and he was shy, very unlike the other Yanks that frequented the milk bar before him. He had tried so hard to mask his limp that I'd known at once that he was based at The Southport School hospital. I couldn't help smiling to myself at his efforts to be whole; most of the other men used their injuries to drum up sympathy. By the time he plucked up the courage to ask me out, he'd almost won my heart, although of course I didn't let him know that.

A lorikeet sailed up and landed next to my hand, so close I was sure I could touch it if I stretched out my fingers. But I didn't, because for a long time now the world had been cold to my touch. Instead, I closed my eyes and pictured James, young and unlined, fit and tanned. Springbrook had become 'our' place, and we had come here often in those early days. We'd picnic and swim, take walks in the rainforest, and climb up here to the top of the waterfall to take in the view below. Soon, through the normal progression of such things, we had started discussing our future.

"Come with me," James had asked. It was raining outside and we were sitting in Mum's tiny lounge room above the shop.

"Stay."

"I can't. You know I can't." He'd reached out and brushed my hair out of my eyes, his touch impossibly gentle and so full of love.

"But I have a family too, a family business. With Dad and both my brothers gone, I need to be here to help Mum with the shop. I know it's not a big fancy bank in America like your family business, but the milk bar is all my family has."

"I'll wait for you, for as long as it takes. I love you."

"I love you too, I do. Please don't ever doubt that. But it's not that simple." I'd stood up and walked towards the window, leaning out and smelling the ozone in the damp air. "You know as well as I do that there's no guarantee I'll even be allowed to travel to America, or how long I'll have to wait for a passage. Jane Stevenson was in the shop this morning, her visa's been denied, Richard's being redeployed, and she has no option but to stay here on the South Coast and wait for something to change. She's pregnant, what is she going to do? I don't want to be in that position. You there, me here, no way for us to be together. And they're married, what chance do we have?"

I felt his strong arms slide around my shoulders as he stood behind me, "I won't let that happen, you know I won't."

I had laughed then, and turned around and kissed him, folding myself into his warm embrace. I was charmed by his sense of invincibility, but I was faced with the reality of the war brides' situation on a daily basis. Jane was not the first, and would certainly not be the last victim.

"What are you doing to do, smuggle me into America in your kit bag?"

He had held me away from him, and looked deep into my damp eyes, "You know they're looking at the laws. Rumour has it there'll be a new law passed any day now which sorts out all this nonsense, makes it easier for all these couples to be together."

"I've heard all that before, but until then the likes of poor Jane are still stranded. I've been through that before, I'll not do it again."

"I'm not Shawn, Pru. I'm not going to go off to war, and leave you. My war is over, my knee has seen to that, I'm not going to go off and die."

My heart lurched at the memory of Shawn, even after all these years, and the lorikeet flew away, as if in sympathy. Shawn had been my first love, and my heart had broken, irreparably I'd thought, when his mum had come around to our place, the crumpled telegram clutched in her fist. Shawn had been her only son, her only child, and we'd cried in each other's arms for hours. That had been three years before James walked into dad's milk bar, when I'd finally realised that time had healed my heart, but not enough to make me put it at risk again.

I'd unwrapped myself from James' embrace, and moved to refill our tea cups, "I know you're not Shawn. But my heart won't survive another heartbreak. I can't help but think that once you get back home, you're going to forget all about me and I'll be left alone again."

James had taken the teapot out of my hands, and stroked my fingers with his strong, calloused hands. "Even if I never lay eyes on you for the rest of my days, I would never forget you. I hope in time you will learn to trust again. Trust me."

Trying to shake the memories, which haunted me, I opened my eyes and cast them down over the pool of water beneath the waterfall, towards the spot on the bank that had been our spot. Oh, how I *had* loved James, how I *had* learned to trust him, how I ultimately *had* invested my whole heart in him, only for it to lead to heartbreak once again. It wasn't him I needed to learn to trust, it was, after all, myself. I didn't even notice the tear rolling down my cheek until it plopped onto the front of my sundress.

James's rehabilitation had taken longer than he'd thought. He'd been injured far more seriously than he'd first let on to me, but I wasn't complaining, because the longer he was based on the South Coast, the longer I believed we would have together.

The seasons changed, and the warm summer cooled to a mild winter. The South Coast was still crawling with American and Australian soldiers sent to the coast to recuperate and rest. James and I were becoming known around town as an item. Because of my pale Irish skin, I didn't spend much time at the beach, but that October of 1945 when the weather was perfectly mild, it was there, at Burleigh, that James struggled to his good knee in the soft sand, and pulled the shiny ring from his pocket.

"If I have to spend the rest of my life traversing oceans or scaling mountains or fighting wars to do it, I will, because I want to spend the rest of my life with you. Will you marry me?"

I had taken the ring, and turned it over in my hands, while James balanced precariously on one knee. Oh, how I had wanted to slip it onto my finger, and hold it up to the sunlight and watch it sparkle. I had wanted to throw my arms around James and tumble into the sand, laughing with joy and happiness, but instead, with a heavy heart, I had handed it back to him.

"I can't. I'm sorry."

"Pru."

"Please, don't make it harder. It's not that I don't want to, I do, but if I say yes, it means that it's over."

"Over?"

"Yes. Then it's over for me. Then I'm totally invested, my hopes, dreams and future rest on you. And me leaving everything I know and coming to America. If I can even get to America. And right now I can't, which means I'll be left here, with everything on the line, you'll go back, and my heart will be broken all over again. I just can't, I can't give in to it all like that."

"Please, just listen to me."

"All right, I'll listen, but you're not going to change my mind."

James had unfurled from his awkward kneel and sat back down on the sand, and taken my hand.

"I want you to think about what we have. You see, I believe that even without this ring, you're totally invested, and even if I go back now, today, your heart will be broken. Because I think, no, I know, that you love me as much as I love you. That you want a life with me, a future. This will only make our chances stronger. You know that wives have higher priority for transport than fiancées or girlfriends. I want us to get married, here, in Queensland, on the South Coast surrounded by your friends and your mum, and we'll do whatever it takes to get you home with me. I can't stay, you know I need to go back, but I will not leave you here. I will stay as long as I need, to make sure that happens."

If I closed my eyes, I could still feel his warm hands on mine, as he had lifted my hand and slipped the ring onto my finger, and at last we had fallen into a tearful embrace.

James and I had gone home to Mum, who was happy for me, despite her concerns. She had seen what I'd gone through when Shawn died, and she knew that James and I faced a difficult path ahead. But she could see that we loved each other.

James and I sat down at the kitchen table and he wrote to his parents, telling them about me, and that we were to be married, and that he'd be returning home with his bride. I blushed as he told them how beautiful I was, how much he loved me, and how he knew they would love me too. He was going to send a telegram the next day when he posted the letter, saying he was getting married and that a letter with more information was on its way. After finishing the letter, and sealing it in one of Mum's envelopes, we sat late into the night talking about the wedding, as I examined and re-examined my pretty ring.

It was going to be a simple affair. James may have been wealthy back in the States, but there was still a war on, and everything was in short supply. But we didn't care, because it didn't matter to us. For weeks we could talk of nothing else.

I stood up and stretched my aching bones, stiff from having sat at the waterfall for so long. A few hikers had passed by, but they hadn't noticed me, nobody did these days. I climbed down and skirted my way around the edge of the pool, remembering a time when I skipped across those rocks, James at my side, young and in love without a care in the world. I settled down in our old spot, my legs folded beneath me, and closed my eyes. Today would have been our sixtieth wedding anniversary, and I unconsciously rubbed my left finger, where once my pretty ring had sat.

By November 1945 our plans were made, we'd set a date for our wedding, the first week in January. Everything was perfect.

James came around to the house one Thursday night, and I knew immediately that he had news. He was quiet all through dinner, distracted, and when he asked me to take a walk with him after dinner, I had a sense of foreboding.

"I've been billeted."

"What? But you're injured!"

"The war's over, but I've been billeted to be transported back to the States. I leave in two weeks."

I was silent, as visions of our wedding melted before my eyes.

"This doesn't change anything."

"It changes everything. It's all happening again."

"No." James had pulled me towards him, looking into my eyes. "Nothing has changed. I won't let it. So we may have to change a few dates around, make sure we're married before I go, but I still love you, that hasn't changed."

"But you promised you wouldn't leave me. You promised you'd wait." I had whispered, my mind swarming, trying to make sense of what he was telling me.

"You know I can't change this. I don't have a choice, but it doesn't change the way I feel about you, or the future we're going to have together. It may happen differently to how we thought, how we planned, but it will still happen, the end result will be the same."

I had shivered, and he had removed his coat and placed it lovingly around my shoulders.

"Please. We'll move the wedding up, and before you know it you'll be on a boat headed for the U.S. To our new life together."

"I can't just leave on the next ship James. I have to help Mum in the milk bar—I can't just leave her alone."

He had walked me back home, and left me with a soft lingering kiss, which reflected our melancholy mood. My hand slid across his shoulder and down across his strong chest, as I turned away and walked through the door, closing it slowly behind me.

In my room I had shrugged off James's jacket which I realised I still had draped over my shoulders, and hugged it to me, inhaling his scent as tears welled in my eyes, and that is when I had felt the sharp corner of the envelope in the pocket. Ordinarily I would never have dreamt of invading James's privacy, but the letter was open already, and postmarked U.S.A.

I'm afraid I'm writing with some bad news, son. While I'd rather speak to you in person, given the news you shared in your last letter, I'm hoping this reaches you before it's too late.

Your father has had a stroke. He is still alive, and somewhat functional, but the truth is that he will not work again and you are urgently needed back home at the bank. Harold Sutherland is holding down the fort until your return, but I urge you to get here as soon as you can. I am sure you can ask for some sort of special dispensation for early release.

Your plans to marry Prudence will obviously need to change. I know you think you are in love, dear, but I'm sure that once you're back home with the family you will realise that this Prudence, while I'm sure she is a lovely girl, is only an infatuation brought about by your war experience and injury. There is a lot of talk here about those Australian women and their reputations, and I'm sure she won't be too disappointed when you break off the wedding. Don't be too disheartened dear, you'll soon find someone infinitely more suitable here, who will be a far better match. But your father and I both agree that Prudence is not the woman for you.

Enjoy your last remaining days in Australia, have fun, as they say, but please be prepared to take on the necessary responsibility upon your return.

I had re-read that letter over and over, trying to make sense of it. Had James lied to me about being billeted? Or was it just an excuse for him to leave me? But then why did he want to bring up the wedding? Or was that a ploy to lead me into a false sense of security? I was so confused, and had lain awake the whole night weeping, clutching the letter.

It was early the next morning when I crept out of the house, and headed up to Springbrook. The sun was just starting to kiss the sky as I trudged up to the top of the waterfall, still in yesterday's rumpled clothes, my eyes swollen with spent tears. I had wanted to clear my mind, to figure out what I was going to do, but I was filled with a whirlwind of emotions I couldn't decipher. I'd collapsed at the top of the waterfall, the letter, now damp and rumpled, clutched in my hand.

I don't remember removing my pretty ring, rolling up the letter and threading it through the gold band. But I remember the shiny stone rolling out of my hands, and down along the jagged rock towards the rushing water below, towards the crystal clear pool below. I'd lurched forward from my position, in a desperate effort to catch it, when the toe of my shoe caught in the hem of my dress and I'd stumbled, and found myself rolling towards the edge of the falls. The last thing I remember is seeing the ring, the letter still neatly threaded like a scroll, caught in a rocky outcrop, safe from the water below, as I tumbled backwards into blackness.

Later, I looked down on the scene from where I was suspended in limbo. There were people all around now, staring at my body as it floated, Ophelia-like in the pool at the bottom of the waterfall, at peace at last. The rolled letter still lay where it had landed, and would soon be discovered and returned to James.

Nobody came to the waterfall for a while after that day, as if it was a cursed place, but I didn't mind having the place to myself. It gave me time to learn to be alone. Then, I received my first visitor, and of course it was James. He had spread a blanket under the tree in our favourite spot, set out two wine glasses and poured each of us a drink. He spoke to me as if he knew I was there, and although I tried to reach out and comfort him, to wipe the large tears which rolled down his unshaven cheeks as he spoke to me, it was clear that he was unaware that I was there, right beside him.

"I should have been more honest with you, my love, but I wish you'd had more faith in me, in my love for you. I wrote back to mother, you see, and told her that I'd been billeted, and was due to sail out in two weeks. But I made it clear to her that I would be marrying you before I left, that I loved you more than anything, and that if she was going to force me to choose—which I'd hoped she wouldn't—that she'd not be happy with the outcome. I know I should have told you about the letter, and I'm sorry I didn't, but you need to know that I didn't want to hurt you, to put more pressure on you because I know how stressed you were already about my early billet. I meant what I said to you, Pru, that even if I never again laid eyes on you for the rest of my days, I would never forget you, and even though we will never be married, there will be a place in my heart forever reserved for you."

I tried to tell him that it was an accident, that I would never have left him that way, but for years afterwards people would come to the falls, and point and tell their visitors of how the heartbroken war bride had flung herself from the falls. No matter what I tried, I came to accept over time that there was nothing I could do to reveal the truth. My only regret is that James will forever be burdened with a guilt that is not his to bear. One day perhaps he will return here, and I will be waiting for him, always.

BREATH

Tara Calaby

When the ghost stories took over the campfire conversation, Ellen Andrews protested mildly, fulfilling her duty as chaperone, but made no real attempt to stop them. Past trips had taught her that a little fear was the perfect way for the girls to work off their excess energy before climbing between their blankets for the night, and a couple of scared ten-year-olds were much easier to handle at three in the morning than a camp full of gigglers, too high on adventure to fall asleep.

Betty Richardson was always the one to start the stories. At fourteen, she was one of the oldest girls in the unit, but she had never been made a Patrol Leader, or even a Seconder, too fond of mischief to be a suitable example to the younger girls. Despite this—or perhaps because of it—she was one of Ellen's favourites. Officially, of course, a Unit Leader didn't *have* favourites, but you couldn't spend hours with a group every week without getting to understand the different personalities and forming the corresponding biases.

Margaret Brown, for instance, was the perfect Patrol Leader. She listened carefully to everything that Ellen said and looked out for the newest members of the unit. Her hair was neat—even in the middle of the bush—she always carried a handkerchief, and she was one of the greatest bores that Ellen had ever known. Her best friend, Rosie, was similarly well-behaved, but had a broad streak of timidity that irritated Ellen to the point of gritted teeth at times. She would happily take the mischief of Betty or the accident-prone daring of Janet over fearfully *good* girls every time.

"This is a true story," Betty said, leaning towards the fire so that the light of the flames cast rippling shadows over her round face. "It happened very near here."

The younger girls fidgeted nervously, and one jumped as a spark flew into the air.

"Now, Betty," Ellen said, smiling reassuringly at her unit, "you know it's just a story."

"It's not, Miss Andrews," Betty protested. "It's true. My brother told me so."

"Your brother isn't a particularly reliable source." Ellen had seen Joe Richardson stumbling out of the Nerang Hotel with red cheeks on many occasions.

"But he is, Miss Andrews. He's ever so smart. Anyway," Betty continued, unperturbed, "this all happened a long time ago, back when the bush stretched all the way down to the store. Nerang barely even existed back then. It was just a few sugar and maize farms, and nothing but trees and scrub and the river in between."

"We've heard this one before," Margaret said, and Rosie nodded beside her. "You tell it every time."

"That's because it happened *right here*," Betty said. "The new girls haven't heard it before, and they need to know the story in case *he* comes to the camp tonight."

"He?" Little Shirley Butlin, fresh out of Brownies, was Betty's perfect audience.

"The ghost of Tamborine!"

Several of the girls moved a little closer to the fire.

Encouraged, Betty continued her tale. "He wasn't always a ghost, of course. He used to be a farmhand called Henry Addison. He worked for one of the first farmers in the area, harvesting the sugar cane and cutting down trees to clear the paddocks. The farmer was greedy and cruel, but Henry kept out of his way as best as he could, and they got along well enough."

"Until the daughter arrived," Janet said.

Betty nodded. "Exactly. The farmer had a daughter, you see. She'd been at school in Brisbane for all the time that Henry had been working at the farm, so he'd never so much as seen her before. But, when they finally met for the first time, they fell instantly in love."

"I thought this was a ghost story," Shirley complained, "not some stupid romance."

"It *is* a ghost story. You see," Betty said, "the farmer didn't think much of his farmhand wooing his daughter. He thought she was too good for a simple harvester like Henry, so he worked out a way to separate the two of them forever. He sent his daughter to her aunt in Brisbane for the weekend, and then lured Henry to the dam by telling him that there was an issue with the water supply. And, when Henry bent over to see what was wrong, the farmer leapt forward and drowned him!"

There was a collective gasp from several fire-lit faces. Even Margaret appeared to be listening now, although she maintained her air of displeasure by keeping her gaze fixed on the fire.

"The farmer told his daughter that Henry had run away with a timber cutter's wife, and she believed him. She cried for a month, and then started taking long walks with the minister's son. The farmer thought the affair was over." Betty smiled. "He was wrong. The very night after the farmer announced the engagement of his daughter, he received a visit from Henry Addison."

"The ghost!"

"The ghost." Betty nodded across the fire at Shirley. "Henry waited until the farmer was sleeping, and then stood over him, dripping dam water onto the floor. He leaned forward and slowly, very slowly, opened his mouth and inhaled.

"In the morning, the farmer was found dead in his bed. The only sign of Henry was a puddle on the floor and the terrified look on the farmer's face. The doctor said that he'd suffocated, but the truth was that the farmer had stolen Henry's breath from him, when he drowned him in the dam, and Henry had finally claimed his revenge."

Janet picked up a long twig that lay at her feet and used it to stoke the fire, sending a spray of sparks into the blackness overhead.

Betty watched as they faded, and then continued her story. "Since that night, Henry has roamed through the bush, appearing every few years to kill again. So if you hear the sound of dripping water, or smell the mud of the dam, you can be sure that the ghost of Tamborine is nearby, waiting for you to fall asleep so he can steal your breath away."

There was a moment of silence as Betty sat back, looking pleased with her performance. Then a green branch snapped loudly from within the fire, and several girls shrieked.

"It's just the fire," Ellen said quickly, before the squeals could turn to tears. "The only ghosts you're likely to see here tonight are the ghosts of all those sausages you ate for dinner. I'll never understand how such small girls can get through so much food."

"It's the hiking, Miss Andrews," Margaret said. "It builds the appetite."

Beside her, Rosie was looking rather pale. As one of the older members of the unit, she had probably heard Betty's tale on at least four other camping trips, but if there was anyone timid enough to jump at shadows on every occasion, it was Rosie Miller. Ellen still remembered the time the girl had fainted at the sight of an engorged leech stuck to one of her knees. Guiding hardly seemed the most suitable activity for her, but there was always the hope that some of Janet's verve might eventually prove contagious.

"How about another story, Betty?" Shirley asked.

"Oh *don't.*" Rosie looked to Ellen for support. "We've had enough of Betty's horrible stories for one night."

"Horrible?"

"I'm sure she didn't mean it like that, Betty," Ellen said. She spent more time preventing squabbles between her Guides than she spent teaching them how to tie knots or leading them on hikes. "Besides, it's getting late, and we have a long walk back tomorrow. It's time you all climbed into your tents."

"Must we, Miss Andrews? It's such a lovely night." Janet gestured broadly to the heavens above them. "Can't we sleep beneath the stars?"

"Oh yes, let's." Margaret clapped her hands in agreement. "There's not a cloud in the sky."

Ellen looked to the younger girls, who were looking a little worried at the thought. "I don't see why you shouldn't sleep in the open if you want to," she said, "but those of you who prefer canvas over your heads may join me in the tents."

Despite her earlier bravado, Shirley was one of the first to claim a tent. Most of the younger girls followed suit, as did Rosie, who ignored Margaret's entreaties in favour of a little more protection against spiders and snakes. Ellen delayed her own bedtime until she had checked the dying fire and ensured the older girls were safe and comfortable in their blankets under the stars, but soon she too was wrapped in scratchy wool and feeling the pleasant sensation of sleep settling upon her.

She was woken by a scream. *Betty*, she thought immediately, but when she untwisted herself from her bedding and clambered out from her tent, Ellen was surprised to see the girl in question looking sleepy and confused as she rose from her own bed on the flattened grass beside the embers of the campfire.

From the colour of the sky, Ellen could tell that dawn wasn't far away. It was a strange time for mischief, but she had spent enough nights with these girls to know that anything was possible. "All right, who was it?" she asked, looking from shadowy face to shadowy face as she searched for any hint of guilt from the culprit.

"It wasn't us, Miss Andrews." Janet pointed toward the line of tents. "It sounded like it came from over there."

"It wasn't me," Shirley said quickly. A brown blanket was wrapped around her shoulders, making her look like an extension of the tent she stood in front of.

"Actually," Margaret said, looking worried, "it sounded a lot like Rosie."

"She probably just saw a spider." Betty shook her head dismissively, and settled back down into her wrap of blankets. "If nothing fun is happening, I'm going back to sleep."

"But if it was just a spider, where is she?" Margaret moved over to Rosie's tent, looking back to make sure that Ellen was following her before she bent and ducked beneath the canvas.

Ellen gestured to the other girls to wait where they were. They were looking more disgruntled than interested now that the screamer had been identified as Rosie, and Ellen wasn't sure that she blamed them. It wouldn't be the first time that Rosie had overreacted to the sight of a tiny spider, although it was certainly the first time she'd managed to wake the entire unit by doing so. Ellen tried very hard to like all of her charges, but sometimes it was a challenge.

As Ellen walked over to meet her, Margaret's head appeared from the darkened triangle of Rosie's tent. "Miss Andrews," she said, her face white, "I think she's dead."

Ellen ran the last few steps. Margaret began to cry as Ellen helped her to her feet. She hugged the girl briefly before passing her into Betty's care and crawling into the shadowy tent. Rosie lay in a cocoon of blankets, her face a pale circle surrounded by messy hair. Her eyes were open, but she didn't move, even when Ellen knocked a knee against her as she dug in her pocket for a match.

The flame lit the tent with an eerie light that reflected off the water-spattered groundsheet. Rosie stared up at the canvas roof above her. Ellen felt her breath catch in her throat. Margaret was right. Rosie was dead.

They hiked out as soon as the sun rose above the horizon. Ellen hated the thought of leaving Rosie there alone, but she had no other choice. Logically, she knew that poor Rosie was past minding, but there was just something so final about covering her motionless body in blankets and leaving her with the charred circle that marked where the fire had been.

The other girls walked in melancholy silence. Ellen had never known them to be so quiet, but she was glad for the lack of conversation. She dreaded their arrival back in Nerang and yet could not find any of her usual enjoyment in the hike through the thick bush of the hinterland. Even the sound of birdsong and the rich scent of decaying leaves did nothing to cheer her. It was a long walk—somehow much longer and more tiring than the chatter-filled outward hike the previous day. It seemed that the bush stretched on forever, but when they finally arrived at the road, noon was still hours away.

The rest of the day was a slow blur of phone calls, policemen and crying girls. Although the Guides' campsite was regularly used by other campers, the police insisted that Ellen accompany them on the trek back through the bush, in case they were unable to locate Rosie on their own. They were joined by Bill Jackson, the local doctor, who puffed and coughed with the exertion of the hike. The gums loomed like bark-draped skeletons on either side of the track and cast ever-darkening shadows as the sun began its downward arc.

When they arrived at the clearing, Ellen waved the men towards the lone remaining tent, but did not follow them. There was a circle of bruised grass around the remains of the campfire, and she sat within it, twisting a string of bark around one finger and trying not to hear the blunt conversation of the policemen.

Jackson was in the tent for a long time. When he emerged, still fastening his bag, his brows were low and his expression grey. "Strange," he said, his voice just loud enough to carry over to where Ellen was sitting. "I've never seen anything like it."

"What do you mean?" The youngest of the policemen peered into the shadowy opening of the tent.

"From what I can tell, the child suffocated. But there's no airway obstruction and no sign of interference." Jackson shook his head. "It's as though something just stole her breath right away."

The bark tore. Ellen stood and walked over to the tent, ignoring the group of men as she pulled the canvas roof free of its wooden posts. The groundsheet was dry now, but when Ellen bent to stroke the hair back from Rosie's face, the scent of muddy water filled her nostrils.

The dark bulk of Tamborine Mountain rose above the canopy of eucalyptus. Ellen straightened and turned away from its ancient gaze.

JUMPINPIN

Thoraiya Dyer

Tim gets breathalysed every morning at the office.

That's how he knows he's not just tanked when he sees the reflection of his hands in the window glass, holding the suction cups ready to pick up the pane, only the hands in the reflection aren't holding any suction cups, and besides, they're too white to be his hands.

In the glass is the transparent ghost of a man, not in blue overalls, the glazier's get-up, but wearing a loose, long-sleeved white shirt, a buccaneer in belted trousers, with a wind-swept, desperate look.

Wind-swept. Yet, where Tim is standing, by the external aluminium glass rack of his van, in the shadow of the shopping centre where a tobacconist with a car-rammed frontage waits for Tim's early morning delivery, there's no actual wind. Only Donut King cups, still as statues, and dewy dandelions growing in the pavement cracks.

The ghost fogs the other side of the glass with his breath and writes in it with his finger. Tim can only stare. His suction cups dangle like the appendages of a sad human fly. There *is* no other side of the glass; no more than a few centimetres between that pane and the one locked into the dampeners behind it.

I've been broken into pieces, the ghost sketches hastily. *Take me back. Please. Take all of me back.*

"Take you back where?" Tim gasps. The ghost breathes silently on another part of the pane.

Stradbroke Island. They buried me on the beach in 1894. Most of my bones still lie in the channel, but some have been mined, with the sand. Now part of me is in the glass. This piece, and the other one.

His long finger traces the place where he's already written: *Please.*

Then he adds:

You've been to the island. You know. You've been to Jumpinpin or you couldn't see me. None of the others could see me.

Tim swallows. His eyes hurt. He's hungover; that has to be it. Drinking, drinking, drinking to forget Kylie Waters. They didn't bring in the breathalyser because they're racist, even though they are, all of them except the boss. They brought it in because he dropped that sheet, that big sheet, outside the Real Estate Agent, jumping at shadows. Scared of nothing.

"It wasn't nothing," Tim exclaims. He kicks a tyre. Swears like a trooper. "You made me drop it. It was you that I saw."

It was me, the ghost admits. *I can't go until I'm all together. First they blew me up with dynamite. Half in the North Island, half in the South. The curlews came to take my spirit on but I couldn't go with them.*

"That's not why," Tim corrects him fiercely. "Curlews can't take you. The land doesn't own you. Not like our mob that your mob killed, a ways back." He imagines the guardians of the departed ones, the brother birds that carry men to the shadow land, picking up this old spirit, only to drop it like a too-hot potato chip, back into the waves of the Pin, the deep sea channel that separates North and South Straddie.

He can't think of the Pin without thinking of Kylie Waters laughing as she hauled up that bream. Dark curls escaped from under her ugly hat, fingernails bright as the bright lures she used; bright as the epileptic fit-inducing lipstick she wore, even on a fishing trip.

Tim crosses his arms over his chest.

"I can't go back up north. I've got work to do. Plus, do you know how much this piece is worth? I can't waste my wages buying big bits of glass to chuck in the Pin for no reason."

You want to go back.

"No, I really don't."

It's the truth, for a whole agonising minute. Tim's well shot of the place where he grew up. All his family, and Kylie's, interfering in his business. Thinking he's too stupid to take care of himself.

North. North, where he'd stood in the underground Odditorium, holding Kylie's hand in the golden glow of Ripley's banknote hologram while tourists in bad T-shirts trod Cavill Street, Surfers Paradise, up above their heads, and Kylie had said about the hologram, *It's beautiful but useless.*

And because she hadn't wanted to move with him to the city, and he'd wanted to hurt her the way he'd been hurt, he'd said the unforgiveable words, *Beautiful and useless, just like you.* He'd gone south on his own, fished the beaches and mudflats without her, pulled up flathead and snapper that never tasted as good.

He does want to go back.

Of course he wants to go back.

The ghost makes him stop by the industrial bin where the broken shards of the other piece of glass have been swept up and tossed in, mingled with plaster and wooden house frame cut-offs.

"Let me get this straight," he says as his gloved hands handle the razor-sharp shards, plucking them out of the bin and into an old plastic paint-bucket. "You were on that *Cambus Wallace*, that old ship that ran aground in a storm, and you tried to swim to shore but you drowned. And then some idiot detonated explosives in the same spot where some other idiot buried you?"

It was a big explosion, the ghost writes in tiny letters on the piece that Tim is holding. *It weakened the structure of the dunes. Then there was a cyclone powerful enough to eat the sand away. The island was split in two.*

"So then, over a hundred years later, half of you gets dug up by bulldozers, your bones turned to dust and mixed in with a bunch of sand at the Vance mine, and you get melted down into glass."

Heat, and pressure. Like you can't imagine.

Tim knows about heat and pressure. What it felt like to be inside Kylie Waters. Why didn't he apologise for what he said? Why too stubborn to meet her halfway?

"I'm a glazier," he says, throwing the glass into the bucket and digging around in the bin for the next piece. "I know how glass is made."

He drives all the way, through the night, without stopping.

In the morning, red-eyed, he's waiting at the Runaway Bay Marina for the charter boat place to open. The one where Kylie Waters works. Everything looks the same—same old seagull motif, multi-storey powerboat parking, all the lime green fan-shapes of the palm and banana trees and the breadfruits with people's initials carved into the soft, sappy boughs.

It's summer. Even this early, heat rises from the bitumen under beastlike, boat-towing four wheel drives. The ghost's reflection doesn't appear in the frontages of the wall-to-wall Real Estate Agencies selling the line: You, Too, Can Live In Paradise; but then, Tim doesn't need to talk to the ghost any more.

He's got the glass. He needs a boat. He'll dump the molten sand back where it came from; back where mother earth intended it to stay, or be moved by her, not by upstart ants crawling all over her, setting off explosions, eating up the inedible with bulldozers, day and night.

People got to eat, Kylie's mum said to him, once. *And not just fish, smarty pants. People need other things besides fish and the sky and the sea.*

Tim stares at the boat charter window, compact as an ice-cream van's, and can't help imagining, in place of the tin shutters, the way that Kylie used to be framed by it, vivid as a picture, long hair and rainbow fingernails spilling over the edges.

In two minutes, she'll open that window.

She'll open the window and see him.

Maybe she'll slam the shutters down, again, without giving him the time of day. Maybe he'll have to get a boat from the other place, the rip-off place, where they won't let him take it without a massive deposit.

Tim checks his watch.

His heart races.

Sounds inside the tin shutters. Scratching. Someone undoing the locks.

The window flies open and it isn't Kylie's face. It's her mum's face, wider, the bushy hair greyer, and with a front tooth broken in the shape of a number seven. Kylie's mum reckons seven is her lucky number and she won't let the dentist touch it.

"Well, well," Kylie's mum chortles. "Look what the mongrel dog dragged in!"

Tim can't say anything for a full minute. He's more afraid of finding out whether Kylie's standing just inside the shop than he is of running errands for ghosts.

"Hey. I just wanted –"

"You wanted a kiss and make up? It's been more than a year, Timothy Jenkins! You really thought she'd still be here?"

His body jolts.

"Where is she?"

She laughs; takes her time, keeps him in suspense, while he stares at her number-seven tooth, trying to make the seconds go faster until she finally decides to tell him. In the end, she doesn't even say it, just writes an address and phone number on a piece of the boat charter company's stationery, holding it out to him to read like words traced in fog by a ghostly finger.

The address is four blocks from the glazier's where he works.

"Right next to me," he says dumbly. "She lives right next to me."

"Got a spot at that university. Clever girl, our Kylie."

"But she said she wanted to stay here."

Kylie's mum winks at him.

"She'll be back. You're back, aren't you? They all come back, in the end. Don't tell her I said this, Timothy, but she can't stay far from you. You're halves of the same whole, aren't you? Known it since you were kids."

Tim puts the precious piece of paper into his wallet and slips it away.

"I'm not back," he says to Kylie's mum. He's got to put the glass where it belongs before he can go on. "Not yet. I need to borrow a boat."

Foam flies through the air and spatters on the honey-coloured sand.

Tim guns the motor and the boat sits up higher than he would like, slapping across the surface instead of digging in deep, but he's against the wind and the tide and there's no other way to get to the place where the ghost is telling him to go.

SLAM, goes the boat in the troughs, jarring his bones in their sockets. SLAM, SLAM, SLAM.

When he looks down into the bucket of shards, shaking the water out of his eyes, the ghost is smiling, or rather, the ghosts are smiling, hundreds of tiny ghosts in hundreds of shards of glass, some of them dusty from the plaster he couldn't separate from the rest, others darkened by the laminate still bridging the cracks.

Six white buckets of glass.

Tim has no way of anchoring in the powerful rush of the Pin. He turfs the first two buckets over the side; knows the other boats are watching him, but maybe they'll think he's chumming.

Then he's a hundred metres from where he's supposed to be, and gunning the motor again until the little ghosts indicate contentment.

Into the channel go two more buckets of glass.

For the final time, the water carries him away. For the final time, he forces the boat back into position.

"Goodbye, ghost," he says as he dumps the last bucket over. "Sorry about the curlews but I'm sure something else will come for you."

Then he lets the water push him back towards the mainland, towards little islands that are formed, and named, and swept away, and forgotten. On the shore of South Straddie he sees the sand pelting the flat leaves of the breadfruit trees, and the ghostly silhouette of a wind-swept man in a long-sleeved white shirt, a buccaneer in belted trousers, leaning against one of the trees.

Tim can't see his face. Can't be sure if his expression's still desperate and wild. Can't even be sure if there are others beside him.

It doesn't matter. He's got a lot of road to cover in his little delivery truck. He's got a big window to pay for in money and, hopefully, a renewed relationship to pay for in pride.

Then, in two years or twenty, he'll be back.

They all come back, in the end, Kylie's mum said.

Curlews watch him go, knowingly.

THE GHOSTS OF MY ANCESTORS

Nicola Tierney

The ghosts of my ancestors sat on a hill. They watched the sea crash against the shore. Listened to the breeze as it blew through the trees. Watched the rise and fall of the sun. Felt the fire beneath their feet burn within the very earth itself and remembered a day long gone when white sails had blown proud against a blue sky.

Their ship had appeared as a speck on the horizon. From its bow they had looked upon an ancient land. A land of a trillion trees all living and breathing. Contentment, oneness with the very spirits themselves could be felt as it lay easy on this ancient land until… a foreign flag was plunged deep into its parched soil.

My ancestors, full of youth and vigor had come from across the seas, from a land so far away, to find a new land and claim it as their own.

They walked upon its soil leaving strange markings in their wake. They poked and prodded it, gathered plants and animals from it and looked in awe upon the vastness of untapped wealth this land kept within its bosom.

But the land only took a fleeting glance at their passing as my ancestors returned from where they had once come. It took no note of the flag still fluttering in the breeze.

As the land lived and breathed as it had always done, no care was given, no thought was thought. What was known was known. What was felt was felt. What was believed was believed. The land lived on oblivious to the flag now whipped into rags. It also did not hear nor did it care of the cry erupting on the other side of the world. A cry that would change its fortunes forever, that would become more than a memory of adventure and glory as my ancestors now, once more, turned their gaze towards the ancient land and recalled its bounty.

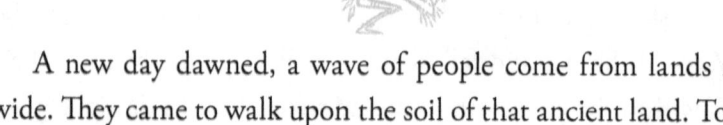

A new day dawned, a wave of people come from lands far and wide. They came to walk upon the soil of that ancient land. To ravage it, to degrade it with their lack of knowledge, understanding and pride.

They sent the destitute, the insane, the murderers to be hidden away from the world behind blocks of rocks. Others, rejoicing in their skill with the blade, carried axes high upon their shoulders and as they made the trees shudder with every blow they extinguished lives that had existed for more than one, two, three thousand years long. They did not hear, nor did they care, how the giants of old screamed.

As the years passed by, as the decades moved on, people came and went like a never ending flowing river, bringing with them death and destruction.

The ancient people of this land were driven out, chained and shackled; many slaughtered to make way for others.

Winding roads appeared in the distance devouring every tree, mountain and river in their path. Humans of all shapes and kinds marched like ants in a row along them as the mass of humanity spread like a plague.

My ancestors grew old and died.

Their offspring now set their eyes, their hearts and their will towards the bounty this ancient land could provide. The tide of humanity could not be turned back.

The ghosts of my ancestors sat on the hill and sighed. Regret for past deeds filled their hearts. They looked for the towering trees of old: the Cedar, the Iron Bark and the Bunya Pine and mourned their loss. They grieved for the loss of the mangroves once filled with crab and fish destroyed with pick and shovel so boats could come closer to shore. They wept for the loss of the wetlands drained so their houses could be built upon it.

They searched for the clouds of birds feeding on the fruiting fig trees. All were gone. The trees felled to make way for steel and concrete to tower in their place. No perch or food were found, no nests could be built. The birds fled to parts unknown.

My ancestor's searched for the cooling streams once filled with fish and prawn. Now the waters lay waste, filled with oil, paint and plastic. Death flowed to the very sea itself.

Where once koala and possum played now tarmac covered the ground.

Where once sacred sites of the peoples of old had marked the land, now all were scattered to the wind, remembered only by the few.

No longer did the animals of old abound in countless numbers. No longer did the air fill with the sound of birds, insects and silence.

Now cars and machines filled the land while planes filled the sky with their never-ending roar. Houses spread like locusts for as far as the eye could see. Roads criss-crossed the land like the webs of spiders. In the distance towering concrete blocks sprouted like mushrooms in one place then another. The very air itself could not breathe, filled with smog and soot.

The land lay exhausted, scarred, despoiled. It had paid a heavy price.

Now the ghosts of my ancestors stood up upon the hill and spread their arms wide and wailed until their hearts broke. Their tears flowed into the sea, their breath drifted on the wind. They called out to the universe, to the energies of the Earth, to the spirits of this ancient land.

"Forgive us for what we have done."

Then some of mankind tilted their heads and turned to look to the hill by the sea. The wind whispered to their hearts and they heard the spirits talk, to call the land back from the brink of destruction. The people then peeled themselves away from their kin, from the vile, the hated... the humans, whose love of man, animal, plant or worm never found a place in their hearts. Only their own existence held meaning to them.

Through blood and bone the rest of mankind heard the spirit of the earth move them to act. To save the forests, few though they be. To save the sea, the running rivers the wild lakes. To clean the waters of plastic, steel and waste. Replant the trees, the forests, the parks. To clear the beaches of the very existence of man.

Only then did the mud crab know it was safe to wash in the salty water of the sea, the eagle to soar, the osprey safe to build its nest. No plastic would fill the stomach of their young now. No fishing line would ensnare their legs leaving them to die.

The trees grew strong and tall and filled the land once more. The birds returned to nest. The fish to breed. The koalas slept the day away as the screech of parrots filled the air that was full of life. The fruit on the vine was sweet to the taste. Flower-scented branches hung heavy as bees buzzed amongst them.

The peoples of old returned. Sacred sites were remembered, revealed and passion flared. The spirit of this land spread through every pore, through every molecule of every being that lived on it, in it and around it.

Then the humans turned once again to the hill by the sea. Drawn towards it, they knew not why. To linger, to walk amongst its trees, to feel its earth beneath their feet, to sit and look upon a rising sun. To laugh, to cry, to feel the joy of the earth as it flowed within them.

The seagulls' cry rang through the air. Laughter drifted on the wind.

Small bare feet ran across the sandy beach as a little girl called with her bright eyes and toothy grin.

"Daddy! Daddy! Come and play."

As I lifted my child up into my arms I turned to the hill by the sea looked up and smiled. The ghosts of my ancestors smiled back.

PHOTO INDEX

All photos have an LS number and have been reproduced with permission and courtesy of the Gold Coast City Council Local Studies Library. All photos can be viewed in high definition, online at Picture Gold Coast, part of the Gold Coast Library's online collections and resources sections.

http://www.goldcoast.qld.gov.au/library

All photos can also be viewed at Prana Writer's website:

http://www.PranaWriters.com

THREE WISHES

pg 49

Wedding portrait of unidentified couple at their Mudgeeraba bush wedding, Queensland, 1924

Photographer: Unknown

THAT GIRL NO MORE

pg 79

Unidentified girl with a 'body board' for surfing, Snapper Rocks, Coolangatta, Queensland circa 1920

Photographer: Unknown

SNAPPER ROCKS

pg 93

View from Rainbow Bay, Coolangatta looking across the Coral Sea with lone surfer in the ocean, to the Surfers Paradise horizon, Queensland, circa 1990

Photographer: Ray Sharpe

WAR BRIDE

pg 201

View of the swimming hole at the base of Twin Falls, Springbrook, circa 1940s

Photographer: Graham Hardy

LS-LSP-CD521-IMG0008

THE CLEARING
pg 59

Twin Falls in the Warrie National Park, Springbrook, Queensland, 1956

Photographer: Ray Sharpe

LS-LSP-CD408-IMG0001

FRANGIPANIS
pg 75

Children feeding lorikeets at Currumbin Sanctuary, Queensland, circa 1980

Photographer: Unknown

LS-LSP-CD1412-IMG001

PULPED FICTION
pg 105

Cars on display at Wharf Street Tweed Heads, Coolie Rocks festival 2013

Photographer: Janis Hanley

LS-LSP-CD1321-IMG013

PULPED FICTION
pg 105

View of Coolie Rocks from Coolangatta Mantra 2013

Photographer: Janis Hanley

EMPTY CALORIES

pg 123

Former cable station – now the music school at The Southport School. Surfers Paradise in the background.

Photographer: Janis Hanley

LS-LSP-CD1412-IMG002

IN THE END

pg 135

Opening of the Infant Saviour Church, Burleigh Heads, Queensland, late 1933 or early 1934

Photographer: Unknown

LS-LSP-CD104-IMG0026

PARADISE DROWNED

pg 153

Jessie Bird's bullock team on the South Coast Road driving past Jim Cavill's original Surfers Paradise Hotel, Queensland, circa 1927

Photographer: Unknown

LS-LSP-CD127-IMG0014

DELIVER ME

pg 171

Delivering bread via a boat which was rowed through flood waters to stranded homes, Waterford, 1947

Photographer: Unknown

LS-LSP-CD098-IMG0069

LS-LSP-CD1034-IMG013

DUCK

pg 183

World War II mobile recruiting unit, Marine Parade, Coolangatta, Queensland, 1941

Photographer: Unknown

LS-LSP-CD1324-IMG001

DUCK

pg 183

Weatherboard beach architecture Mermaid Beach still surviving in 2012

Photographer: Janis Hanley

LS-LSP-CD522-IMG0002

DEAR SAM

pg 193

Looking out through the natural archway formed by Cave Creek undercutting the soft volcanic rock at Natural Bridge, Springbrook National Park, Queensland, 1959

Photographer: Ray Sharpe

LS-LSP-CD331-IMG0007

BREATH

pg 213

Girl Guides eating a meal prepared while on camp on the South Coast, Queensland, circa 1930s

Photographer: George A. Jackman

JUMPINPIN

pg 223

Jumpinpin, South Stradbroke Island,
Queensland, circa 1890

Photographer: Unknown

LS-LSP-CD064-IMG0118

GHOSTS OF MY ANCESTORS

pg 231

View along beach to Burleigh
Headland, 2012

Photographer: Janis Hanley

LS-LSP-CD1323-IMG008

BIOGRAPHIES

Authors

Originally from Kansas City, **TOM BETTS** graduated from the UC Santa Barbara and dabbled in sitcom writing in L.A. He moved to the Gold Coast 27 years ago and has continued scriptwriting and acting. Tom works at Bond University. He and his wife Robyn have three children and two dogs.

KATHLEEN BLEAKLEY has significant Gold Coast history: visiting family, beaches & valleys. Widely published including: *Etchings; Going Down Swinging; Griffith Review; Hecate; Melaleuca; Poetrix; Wet Ink; Windmills; jumping out of cars*, prose, poetry & photography with andrea gawthorne & 'pling; and *Passionfruit & Other Pieces*, writing & etchings with Hannah Parker.

S. ELLIOT BRANDIS was raised on the Gold Coast, but has since escaped to Brisbane. He enjoys humidity, Bloody Marys, public transport, and cowboy hats. In 2014 he will publish his first novel, *Irradiated*, a tale of two sisters living in Brisbane, post-civilisation. http://selliotbrandis.com.

TARA CALABY is a British-Australian author who lives in Melbourne but escapes north to the Gold Coast whenever she can manage it. A classicist and historian by education, her greatest love when writing is to take the familiar and twist it into something new. http://taracalaby.com.

J. S. CHOINSKI is an explorer of fiction in digital frontiers. Her entry for 2012's NaGaDeMo, *Circa Regna Tonat*, an interactive text game, was featured by industry notables Porpentine (*Howling Dogs*), Auntie Pixelante (*Dys4ia*) and Free Indie Games (www.freeindiegam. es). She is excited about the new possibilities provided by combining storytelling and technology.

PENNER CHOINSKI writes to escape and reads in order to escape writing. Choinski has taught storytelling and performed and is a founding Prana Writers member. Choinski's first novel *The Cul-de-sac* delves into Gold Coast suburbia. Following that is *Up There*, about the mysterious disappearance of a woman climbing Mount Everest.

JANE DOWNING has had short stories and poetry published in Australia and beyond. She also has a Doctor of Creative Arts degree from the University of Technology, Sydney.

THORAIYA DYER is a NSW-based science fiction and fantasy writer with a brother-in-law in Parkwood and fond childhood memories of Surfers. Winner of three Ditmar and three Aurealis Awards for her short fiction, her stories have appeared in *Clarkesworld*, *Apex* and *Cosmos* magazines. http://thoraiyadyer.com.

REBECCA FRASER enjoys writing across all genres, with a particular interest in dark speculative fiction. To keep her muse in life's essentials she copywrites for the corporate world, but her true passion lies in bringing words to life through storytelling. Her work has appeared in several magazines and anthologies. http://rebeccafraser.wordpress. com/

PAUL GARRETY is a registered yoga teacher and has recently qualified as a Yoga Therapist. He enjoys bushwalking and meditation and lives in Tugun. The author of two novels, *The Seventh Wave* and *The Emerald Tablets* (Harper Collins-Voyager, 2011) he is currently completing his third novel, and, as always, planning the next.

KAY GIBB was born in South Africa and has lived on the Gold

Coast for five years. Kay was a recipient of one of the places in Gold Coast City's 'Write that Book' program in 2009, and is a member of Prana Writers. www.kaygibb.com

JANIS HANLEY is a writer and strategist with a particular passion for heritage, museums and community education. She enjoys writing to speculate about the future we are creating for ourselves and our planet. Janis is a founding member of Prana Writers. She conceptualised and coordinated the Gold Coast Anthology project. http://JanisHanley.com

JOCELYN HAWES lives in Brisbane. She writes in many genres including playwriting, crime, romance and books for children. Family history is another interest especially stories about the Gold Coast. She enjoys bushwalking. Visits to the Natural Arch provided the inspiration for 'Dear Sam'.

ELLI HOUSDEN loves short stories, reading and writing them. She has flirted with crime writing and penned a few published poems. Elli has edited two anthologies of short stories for schools, and written several English textbooks for Australian schools, as well as being a regular book reviewer for *The Courier-Mail*.

S. G. LARNER (@StaceySarasvati) is a denizen of Brisbane, Australia, where she wrangles three children and explores the dark underbelly of the world in her works. Her work has appeared in *Aurealis*, among other places. http://foregoreality.wordpress.com

BRITT MELVILLE is a freelance copywriter whose love of words and storytelling means she never really has to 'go to work'. Originally from Brisbane, she now lives on the Gold Coast with her young family. www.missword.com.au

Born in Central Queensland, **DI MORRIS** spent her childhood reading, wandering in the bush, and playing piano. She holds degrees in Teaching, Ethnomusicology and Creative writing. Semi-retired now, her many interests include photography, handwriting analysis, literature, music, writing, cloud appreciation and exploring the natural diversity of the Scenic Rim.

BETSY ROBERTS is a Gold-Coast based writer, with competition winning stories published in *All that Glitters* and *Vacations & Travel*. She has been a local librarian for many years, and is currently working to evoke the lost world of her 50's and 60's Coastal childhood in a novel.

DAVID STRINGER is a New Zealand born writer resident in the Gold Coast. Apart from the story 'Three Wishes' he has also written a novel, *Islands of the Heart,* which is currently submitted to an American publishing house. An essay he wrote for the ABR-Calibre Competition in 2012 made the long-list of 20 out of 200 entries. http://www.islandsoftheheart.com

NICOLA TIERNEY met, in 2005, Jeff Gilberthorpe, of the Icon Collection who encouraged Nicola to write about the fantasy creatures inhabitting the miniature village she is building out of gourds. Is a founding member of Prana Writers and has completed her first novel and is working on two more.

Cover Artist

SHAUNA O'MEARA is a writer and artist based in Canberra, Australia. She has contributed the cover and interior art to several Australian speculative fiction anthologies and recently completed the artwork for a short comic commissioned by *Midnight Echo* magazine. In 2013, she placed in the illustrious Writers of the Future competition and has just completed her first novel. http://www.theshauna-corner.wordpress.com/